Manhattan Babies

Three wealthy New York siblings go from boardroom to baby!

The McCallans are one of the richest families in New York.

Elder brother Jacob, rebel Seth and free-spirited Sabrina know all about family ties and the responsibilities that come with running a business.

But now they're all about to have their lives turned upside down by three *tiny* surprises!

Read Jake's story in

Carrying the Billionaire's Baby

Available now!

And look out for Seth's and Sabrina's stories

Coming soon!

Dear Readers,

Welcome to Manhattan...

Or at least the little corner of it run by the McCallan family. Jake the eldest, Seth the rebel and Sabrina the free spirit are only trying to make lives for themselves in a world of old money, society matrons and scandalous pregnancies.

In *Carrying the Billionaire's Baby*, Jake has endured a lifetime of his dad's cruel and capricious discipline to rise to the ranks of chairman of the board of the family business. Now he's the most cautious man on the planet.

Avery Novak calls him stuffy...but sexy. An associate at the law firm that handles his family's legal problems, she runs into him in a coffee shop on Valentine's Day. Because both are dateless, they decide to have dinner and end up sleeping together.

A few weeks later, there's a baby on the way. How will a woman who mistrusts wealthy people ever raise a child with a man who takes privilege as his due?

The McCallans are rich, entitled and scarred by secrets and lies. You won't want to miss a minute of their journeys to happily-ever-after.

Happy reading...

Susan Meier

Carrying the Billionaire's Baby

—

Susan Meier

ISBN-13: 978-1-335-13523-0

Carrying the Billionaire's Baby

First North American Publication 2018

Copyright © 2018 by Linda Susan Meier

Recycling programs
for this product may
not exist in your area.

ISBN-13: 978-1-335-13523-0

Carrying the Billionaire's Baby

First North American publication 2018

Copyright © 2018 by Linda Susan Meier

Printed in U.S.A.

www.Harlequin.com

Susan Meier is the author of over fifty books for Harlequin. *The Tycoon's Secret Daughter* was a Romance Writers of America RITA® Award finalist, and *Nanny for the Millionaire's Twins* won the Book Buyers Best Award and was a finalist in the National Readers' Choice Awards. Susan is married and has three children. One of eleven children herself, she loves to write about the complexity of families and totally believes in the power of love.

Books by Susan Meier

Harlequin Romance

The Princes of Xaviera

Pregnant with a Royal Baby!
Wedded for His Royal Duty

The Vineyards of Calanetti

A Bride for the Italian Boss

Mothers in a Million

A Father for Her Triplets

Single Dad's Christmas Miracle
Daring to Trust the Boss
The Twelve Dates of Christmas
Her Brooding Italian Boss
A Mistletoe Kiss with the Boss
The Boss's Fake Fiancée
The Spanish Millionaire's Runaway Bride

Visit the Author Profile page
at Harlequin.com for more titles.

For my friend, Di.
My partner in crime on the golf course.

Praise for
Susan Meier

"Meier sucked me into this remarkable love story
from the first page and I could not put it down...a
captivating love story."

—*Goodreads* on *A Mistletoe Kiss with the Boss*

CHAPTER ONE

JACOB MCCALLAN STRODE down the quiet hall of Waters, Waters and Mont–gomery—the law firm employed by his family—with tall, lanky Pete Waters, senior partner.

"So, how's your mother holding up?"

Jake glanced at Pete, not surprised he'd asked. His father had died five months before and everyone was worried about his mom. "She's working to pull herself together. Some days are better than others."

"Rumor has it she headed the last board of directors meeting."

Jake grimaced. Nobody was supposed to know about that, but Pete had sources everywhere. Jake chose his words carefully. "She tried."

"Tried?"

"It was no big deal. She walked into the meeting saying she wasn't ready to be put out to pasture and would assume Dad's role as chairman of the board. I took her out of the conference room and privately told her that the corporate bylaws name the CEO as acting chairman."

"You."

He nodded. "Me. I told her that if we went against the bylaws, we risked being sued by shareholders."

"How'd she take it?"

"She was a bit confused. A bit hurt. I think she believed taking over as chairman would give her something to do now that Dad's gone."

Pete took a long, slow breath and blew it out in a gust. "That's rough."

Painter's scaffolding crowded the end of the private corridor to Pete's office. He pointed to the right. "We'll go the long way."

The "long way" took them past cubicles filled with workers on the phone or frantically typing on computer keyboards, then a file room. A wall of windows exposed rows of files—thinner than they had been before most things were stored on computers—and five copy machines.

Jake frowned and slowed his steps. *Was that Avery Novak standing in front of one of those copy machines?*

He couldn't really tell because the tall redhead's back was to him. But a man didn't forget silky hair long enough to tickle his chest when she straddled him.

He told himself to keep walking. He and Avery had had a short fling, which she'd mercifully broken off after three weeks. They'd been dynamite in bed. But out of bed? They would have done nothing but argue about politics and principles if Jake had ever risen to any of her bait. The woman was ridiculously headstrong, and she didn't like rich people.

No matter how hot they were together, he had looked down the board and seen a future filled with her being critical of his privileged lifestyle, and in general acting as if he were Marie Antoinette and she was a beleaguered peasant. His only regret was that *he* hadn't been the one to break it off.

Jake and Pete were just about at the end of the long glass wall, when she turned. Her huge green eyes widened. Her mouth fell open and she quickly lowered the file she held to her stomach. But it was too late. He'd seen the baby bump.

Baby bump!

She had to be at least five months pregnant. Maybe six.

Oh, God... Six?

That took them back to February—when they were dating.

That could be his baby. *His child.*

He glanced at Avery again. Her figure hadn't changed much except for the baby bump, yet she'd looked more womanly, more attractive. He remembered her soapy and sexy in the shower, added the baby bump to the naked body he knew so well, and something raw and emotional ripped through him. Stronger than lust, more profound than awe that they'd created a child, the feeling rendered him speechless. The reality that that "bump" could be *his child* slammed into him like an eighteen-wheeler, mostly because his father had been a terrible parent. He had no idea how a good dad behaved. What a good dad did—

But, no. It couldn't be his child. Avery would have told him. Wouldn't she?

He and Pete finally walked past the file room. Pete still chatted on about Jake's mother. "I understand that she's on shaky emotional ground. But you really have to hold the line with her coming into the business and trying to do things."

"Actually, I'm thinking of giving her a job."

"What?" Pete stopped walking.

Jake stopped too. "She lost her husband." A movement from the file room caught his eye and he glanced up in time to see Avery racing away. His throat constricted. His gut clenched.

Why run away from him if that wasn't his child?

Embarrassment?

Maybe.

Had to be.

She was probably embarrassed she'd found another man and gotten pregnant so soon after him. Because it couldn't be his baby...

Otherwise she would have told him.

He faced Pete. "Mom's grieving. She's searching for meaning in her life. Trying to be chairman of the board proves she wants something to do. Why not give her something?"

"Because she's been a socialite for forty years and doesn't have any skills?" Pete sighed. "Jake, giving her a job is only going to make your life difficult. There are better ways to handle her grief than having her underfoot."

"I'm not sure I agree. Maybe she has skills we don't know about? Or maybe she won't even want a job? At least if I ask, she'll feel wanted."

"I think you'll be sorry."

"Perhaps. But I think I should ask. She's leaving today for a week in Paris. I thought if I offered her something, it would perk her up enough that her friends could snap her out of her depression."

"You're sure she's going?"

"She and her girlfriends have been spending the first week of September in Paris for decades." He took a brief glance up the hall, but Avery was gone. "She'll recognize she needs to be with her friends and go. Besides, there's a charity ball over the weekend that I'm attending this year. She won't miss my first time there and a chance to introduce me to her friends."

"What if she jumps on your job offer and doesn't care about going to the event?"

"A condition of her coming to work for us will be that she takes the week in Paris first."

Pete shrugged as if grudgingly agreeing with Jake's decision.

They reached Pete's office and Jake took one final glance up the hall. He didn't see Avery, but his chest tightened anyway.

As Pete droned on about fulfilling the bequests in his dad's will, Jake realized three things. First, Avery was independent enough that she could consider it her right not to tell him about his own child. Second, if that baby really was his, he was in trouble. He had no idea how to be a parent and he would need all the time he could get to figure it out before the baby was born. Which meant, number three, he was going to have to confront her.

Today.

* * *

Avery didn't get home until after nine that night. Law firm associates did all the paperwork and the bulk of the legwork on most cases. Before she'd gotten pregnant, she'd fought for the extra work. She sat in on every meeting they'd permit her to attend, and campaigned to be a part of every important case. She had a plan, with big goals, and had only allowed herself five years to get the experience she would need to start her own law firm back home in Pennsylvania. She'd had to cram in everything she could.

Then she'd started hooking up with Jake. It was wrong. From day one, she'd known it was wrong. Her dad had gone to jail for something he hadn't done because a rich employer had used his money and influence to ride roughshod over the system, and her dad couldn't afford high-priced counsel to fight him. That was why she'd become a lawyer— to be a voice for people who couldn't pay five- hundred dollars an hour to defend themselves from something they hadn't done. She couldn't date someone just like the guy who'd sent her dad to prison.

No matter how sexy Jake was, an undercur- rent of privilege ran through his life. Riding in his limos, taking his helicopter to Maine for lobster, sleeping in a penthouse monitored by security guards only reminded her that people like Jake didn't know a damned thing about real life, about suffering and struggle…about being normal.

She didn't want her baby getting lost in the shuffle of drivers, maids and nannies, any more than she wanted her little girl or boy growing up thinking money somehow made her better, even as he or she stayed behind a wall of bodyguards, rode in bulletproof limos and lived with the threat of being kidnapped.

She also didn't want to risk the consequences if Jake found out her dad was an ex-con. He could demand that she stay in New York—away from her dad—or even try to take the baby. Then she'd have no way of shielding her child from the craziness of the McCallan life.

So, she'd made the decision not to tell Jake she was pregnant to protect her child. Immediately, relief had coursed through her. Joy at becoming a mom had blossomed. With Jake out of the picture, she was ready to become a parent. Sure, it changed her plans a bit. She'd be returning to Pennsylvania two years sooner than she'd thought, and without sufficient experience, but she'd adapt. She wanted this baby enough that she'd change her life any way necessary.

She kicked off her subway shoes, tossed her briefcase on a chair and headed to her bedroom, but her doorbell rang.

Closing her eyes in misery, she muttered, "Damn it."

She could ignore the bell, but she had a sneaking suspicion Jake McCallan had been sitting in a limo somewhere down the street from her building, waiting for her to come home. He'd seen her that morning. Seen the baby bump. Stickler for detail that he was, he'd undoubtedly done the math.

The bell rang again.

She headed for the door, shaking off her fears. Lawyers planned for all contingencies. Her first choice might have been not to tell him, but that didn't mean she didn't have a backup plan, a Plan B. He was a super-stuffy aristocrat, who wouldn't want a crying child in his world. All she had to do was remind him that a baby didn't fit into his well-ordered life and he'd back off.

Wondering how such a serious, stuffy guy could be so good in bed, she walked to the door and opened it.

"Jake. How nice to see you."

It *was* nice to *see* him. He had black hair cut

short to be neat, but strands poked out, making him look sexy and interesting. His solemn blue eyes always made her want to tell him a joke. But his body was a work of art. He could be an advertisement for the gym. Going three days a week had virtually turned him into a god. And the sex? Amazing. Just thinking about it made her weak-kneed and breathless.

He pointed at her stomach. "That's my baby, isn't it?"

She opened the door a little wider, urging him inside. "Nothing like a little small talk to warm up a room."

He stayed right where he stood. "There's no point to small talk. We have nothing to say to each other, except to discuss whether you're keeping my child from me."

"I'm not. Technically, I'm keeping a pregnancy from you."

He cursed.

"See? This is exactly why I didn't tell you!" She caught his arm and dragged him inside, leading him to one of the two teal-and-white trellis-print club chairs in front of her marble tile fireplace. Though the legs that carried her across the dark hardwood floors were extremely tired, she walked into the kitchen and took a glass from the first white cabinet then filled it at the sink in the center island. Bringing it into her living room, she said, "I knew you'd freak."

He took the water. "I'm not freaking. I'm in shock. You've known about this for months. I just found out today—and only because I ran into you. Not because you told me."

"Okay," she soothed, sitting on the white sofa across from him, keeping control of the conversation. She had to be calm, rational and appeal to his love of order in his life.

"What do you want to know?"

He looked up at her, his gorgeous blue eyes serious, direct. "How?"

She laughed. "I think you pretty much know the basics of how babies are made."

"No. How did you get pregnant? You told me you were on the pill."

The insinuation that the pregnancy was her fault rattled through her like an angry wind, but she gave him a little leeway because he was still processing all this.

"My doctor blamed the antibiotic she gave me for bronchitis. You and I met—" At a coffee shop on Valentine's Day, both dateless and treating themselves to a latte. They recognized each other from the law firm and had an impromptu dinner where he was just so charming and sexy they'd ended up in bed. "—when the bronchitis was all but gone from my lungs." She shrugged. "But while I was celebrating feeling better, I was also finishing up the meds and forgot the antibiotic's effect on birth control."

He set his untouched water on one of the coasters she had on the glass coffee table by the club chair. "I never thought to ask about antibiotics."

Her heart did a crazy little flip. Every time she was ready to write him off as sanctimonious, he'd do something like that. Something that would make her wonder if deep down he was fair. But she knew better. A man with enough money to buy his way into or out of anything had no reason to look at the other side of a situation.

Still, he hadn't blamed her for the pregnancy, so she could go back to Plan B, remind him of how much trouble a baby could be and let him bow out gracefully.

"My goal had always been to get a job at a big law firm and buy a nice condo that would go up in value as I paid down the mortgage."

His earnest blue eyes stayed on her face, as he waited for her to explain why she was rehashing things he already knew.

She cleared her throat. "What I didn't tell you was, I'd made that plan so that I could get tons of experience and learn from some of the best lawyers in the world before I sold the condo for a profit and returned to Pennsylvania to start my own law firm."

"Oh."

She wasn't surprised that she'd stunned him. Every damned time they'd gone out she'd said or done something that raised his eyebrows or caused him to frown. Their problem wasn't merely a case of a middle-class woman with an upper-class man. They were opposites in just about every way.

"I didn't really keep that from you."

"Like you didn't really keep the pregnancy from me?"

She sighed. "We dated for three weeks. There's no law that says I had to tell you my plans for the future."

"So, you weren't seriously dating me. What was I? Beefcake?"

The way he said it, with his calm, poised tone, as if he didn't realize how funny he sounded, made her laugh.

He glared at her. "No. Come on. I'm curious. Did you just go out with me because we were good in bed?"

"You were pretty good."

He cursed and rose from the teal chair to pace. "Seriously!"

"You do realize another man would be so

damned complimented by that he'd probably glow in the dark."

"I'm not like most men."

No kidding. "Okay. Why did you continue to ask me out when we both realized on our third date that we weren't compatible?"

He took a patient breath, but ran the fingers of both hands through his hair. A gesture she'd never seen. She pulled back a bit. The last thing she wanted to do was anger one of the richest men in New York City when she didn't have a leg to stand on to keep their baby from him. Her moving to Pennsylvania without telling him would have been the easiest thing for both of them. But now that he knew, convincing him he didn't want to be part of this baby's life was her best option. She'd never do that if they continued to argue over pointless things.

"Anyway," Avery said, bringing them back to the real discussion. "My life plan has been altered a bit. With my down payment on this place and the extra I've put on the mortgage every month, not to mention the increase in real estate values, I can sell the condo early and still make a profit. Then once I pass the Pennsylvania bar, I can start my own firm there."

"If you wanted your own law firm or even

to jump the ranks of Waters, Waters and Montgomery, all you had to do was say the word."

She gaped at him. "Really? You think it would be okay for me to jump over the heads of lawyers who know ten times what I know? To be made partner before them because my ex is their biggest client?"

He drew a breath and expelled it quickly. "So, you're really leaving?"

Another thing he had a habit of doing was not answering her questions, but changing the subject so they wouldn't argue. This time she appreciated his stopping them from going down another useless road, so she let that slide too.

"Well, I'm not packing up and heading out tomorrow. My doctor is here in New York. I plan to have the baby here. Plus, I have to sell the condo. And I do need the experience I'm getting at Waters, Waters and Montgomery. But eventually I have to go."

"And you expect me to be okay with that?" When he faced her, his sapphire eyes had gone from serious to furious. "You think I don't have rights, options?"

Fear raced through her, but she calmed it. This was the most rational man on the planet. If she stayed neutral, he'd stay neutral. If she set out her plan logically, especially highlighting how he benefited from it, he would follow it.

"Okay, let's start this over again. I am pregnant. The baby is yours. I've had the goal since high school to earn a law degree, get some experience in New York City and then return to Pennsylvania to start my own law firm. The baby doesn't stop that plan. Yes, I have to take the Pennsylvania bar exam and, yes, I will have to get a job at another law firm in Pennsylvania while I study for it. But the goal hasn't changed. Isn't going to change. That's nonnegotiable."

He paced in front of the fireplace. "And, realistically, Pennsylvania isn't that far away. I can drive there to visit or send a limo to bring the baby to me."

She winced. There were a billion things wrong with his idea. Especially considering she didn't want her child sucked into "Mc-Callanville," a world of pampered rich people who didn't understand reality.

She argued the easiest point. "I'm not putting my baby into a limo alone."

"There will be times he should be with me."

"With you? Don't you mean with a nanny? Even when you're home you're on the phone or computer." Just thinking about it filled her with anger. "Why should my baby spend his time with a driver and a nanny when he or she could be with me? I won't let my child be raised by a nanny, Jake. Not ever."

He closed his eyes and shook his head, obviously controlling his temper. Finally, he said, "How much?"

"How much what?"

"How much do you want to make you more agreeable?"

She gaped at him. "Are you trying to bribe me?"

"I'm trying to make you more agreeable."

"And you think if you give me a few hundred or even a few thousand dollars, I'll give you what you want in a visitation agreement?"

"I was thinking more like a few million."

Her eyes widened. "You're insane! I have a plan. I don't need your money! I don't *want* your money. I want to do what's best for the baby. So should you."

He studied her. She could all but see the wheels turning in his head as he came to terms with the fact that this situation wasn't about money. In his world, everything came down to money. She couldn't even fault him for trying to find her price—though she did want to deck him. The truth was, she didn't even want child support. But she figured it was a little too early in the game to tell him that. His brain would have to work so hard to process it that he'd probably have a stroke.

"We're going to need a written agreement."

For ten seconds, she wished he hadn't seen her that morning at the law office. But while her dad had been in prison for something he hadn't done, she learned wishing for things to be different didn't change them. Plus, she hadn't given up on Plan B, convincing him he didn't want a crying, pooping, spitting-up baby destroying the peace of his life. And that would take more tact and diplomacy than she could muster tonight.

"Okay. But we should have a few more conversations to see what we both want before we even try to get anything on paper."

He considered that. "Agreed."

He headed for the door. Though Avery gave him a pleasant smile as she saw him out and said goodbye, another alternative jumped into her brain.

If she couldn't make him see a baby didn't fit into his life, there was a risky Plan C. She could tell him that her dad had been in prison and remind him of the can of worms that would be opened once the press started digging into the life of the woman pregnant with his child. They both knew he wouldn't want that kind of media attention any more than she did. If anything would send him scurrying away from her, it would be the horror of that much negative attention from the press.

There was just one little problem with Plan C—

When she told him about her dad, she'd also be handing him the ammunition to take her child, or to at least keep her and her little one in New York City. All he would have to do would be tell the court he wanted to keep his child away from Avery's ex-con dad.

Then even if she kept custody, she'd be stuck in New York, away from the people she wanted to help.

Away from the dream she had nurtured and worked for since she was fifteen.

If Plan C went south, it could ruin her life.

CHAPTER TWO

THE NEXT MORNING, a quick knock on Jake's office door brought his gaze up from the documents on his ornate mahogany desk, the desk that had once belonged to his dad. Because the list of people his secretary would let down the corridor to his office was slim, mostly family, he automatically said, "Come in."

His brother Seth opened the door and poked his head inside. As tall as Jake and with the same dark hair, Seth hadn't gotten their mom's blue eyes, and had irises so brown they were almost black. Especially when he got angry.

"I won't ask you if you're busy. I know you are, but can I have five minutes?"

Jake sat back on his soft leather office chair. "Sure. What's up?"

Seth walked to the seat in front of the desk. "Just curious if you're really going to offer Mom a job. I mean, it would be kind of fun to watch, but there are twelve people on the board who don't want us giving an office and a paycheck to family members who aren't actually coming into work."

"Since when did you start caring about what the directors think?"

Seth winced. "Since they began calling me because they don't want to insult you by questioning your judgment."

"The way they used to call me when they wanted to complain about Dad—"

He left the sentence open, giving Seth the opportunity to mention if the directors had told him anything about their father, a man whose business practices had been so sketchy they'd teetered on the edge of illegal. Ten years had given Jake a chance to fix most of their dad's messes, to argue him into working fairly or to quietly go behind the scenes and make amends with contractors their dad had threatened to ruin. But Jake didn't want his brother, his sister and especially not their mother to know what a cheat and a thief Tom McCallan had been. Not to preserve their dad's reputation, but to finally shake it off. He didn't want to remember that his dad had emotionally abused him and Seth until his brother had all but dropped out of their family. He didn't want to remember the times his father had publicly humiliated him. He just wanted to get on with his life.

Seth didn't say anything, and his facial expression remained casual.

Jake breathed a silent sigh of relief. Obviously, with Tom McCallan gone the directors believed as he did: the past was the past. It was time to move on.

He caught Seth's gaze. "Pete Waters doesn't like the idea of me hiring Mom either. He thinks she'll be underfoot and that she doesn't have any real skills. But I had a talk with her this morning. I told her there might be a possibility of a job, but she really had to work."

Seth winced. "How did she take that?"

"I think she felt becoming chairman of the board was her due, and a job, though interesting, is a step down." He shook his head. "I'm hoping that going to Paris will make her see she doesn't want any of it. That she's useful enough working with her charities."

"That'll make the board *and* Pete happy."

Jake sighed and sat forward on his chair again. "Speaking of Pete, there's something else I have to tell you."

"About Pete?"

"No. About the lawyer I was dating from his office."

Seth grinned. "The hot redhead."

Jake grimaced. It was typical of Seth to judge a woman by looks alone. Though he had to admit Seth had hit the nail on the head with his description of Avery. She *was* hot, and talking to her the night before had made his head spin. Especially, looking at her stomach and knowing that baby was his. Feelings he'd never before felt had grabbed his chest and squeezed until he couldn't ask the things he should have asked. Like for a DNA test and a good explanation about why she'd kept her pregnancy from him.

"Yes. She's pregnant."

Seth's mouth fell open. "Holy hell. And the baby's yours?"

"She says it is."

"No DNA test?"

He wasn't about to tell his brother he'd turned into a ball of confusion the night before just looking at Avery's belly. He wasn't that kind of guy. He might have had a moment of pure emotion but that was only because he'd been surprised. He was back to his usual controlled self now.

"We ran into each other at a coffee shop on Valentine's Day because neither one of us had a date. She works eighty hours a week. Most of our time together started after nine. It's very clear she doesn't go out with many men. Besides, I trust this woman. She wouldn't lie about something like this."

And that was the bottom line. He did trust her. Not because she was honest, but because the last thing she'd want was more involvement with him or his life. She'd made that abundantly clear. If this baby wasn't his, it would have been her joy to tell him that.

"What are you going to do?"

"First, we need a halfway decent custody agreement."

"What do you think that's going to cost?"

"She doesn't want money."

Seth burst out laughing. "Seriously?"

"She's a lawyer. She can earn her own. Plus, she made a smart choice when she bought her condo. Her plan is to move back to Pennsylvania where the cost of living is a lot lower than what we have here." He shrugged. "There's no price for her. She doesn't need our money."

"Mom's going to have a fit."

"No kidding. Especially since Avery's got to be six months along." He remembered her swollen with his child, and suddenly imagined a little boy that was his. Not just an heir, but someone to teach everything from throwing a spiral to getting what you want in a negotiation. He never thought he'd have a child. Never thought he *wanted* a child. But he needed an heir, and he *wanted* to be a dad. If nothing else, he wanted to do better than his father had done with him and Seth. And come hell or high water he intended to be part of this baby's life.

Seth laughed. "Six months and she only told you now? This just keeps getting better. You should rent an arena and sell tickets for when you tell Mom."

"Very funny."

Seth sat back. "I'm going to be an uncle."

Jake met his brother's gaze. "I'm going to be a dad." Confusion swam through him again, tightening his chest with a combination of elation and fear. For as much as he longed to right things with this child, he also realized he could screw up worse than their dad had.

Seth sighed. "It's official. We're adults. I got word today on Clark Hargrave buying my share of the investment firm we started. He's pulled the money together. Once it comes through, I'm out of the investment business."

"Really?" Jake sat back. "Does that mean you can permanently take over the CEO position I left to become chairman of the board?"

"Do I have a choice?"

"You've been doing the job since Dad died, but if you want to leave I could appoint Sabrina." Both Seth and their baby sister Sabrina had MBAs, but while Seth had started his own company, refusing to work for their dad, Sabrina currently ran a consulting firm for start-ups.

"And ruin her life too?" Seth rose. "I'll do it, but I'm hiring two assistants and a vice president, so I'm not chained to my desk the way you are."

"It's a deal." Jake rose too, extending his hand to his brother.

Seth shook it. "I think we're both crazy."

Considering workload alone, Jake would have agreed with him, except he liked who he was. He had been grateful for the chance to fix the reputation of McCallan, Inc. Now that he had a baby on the way, getting it right was a thousand times more important. He would make his child a part of everything he had—

Unless Avery Novak disappeared. And she just might. They hadn't gotten anywhere close to agreement the night before, and she was just offbeat enough to think running was the answer.

He couldn't bribe her.

He didn't think he could outwit her. They were an even match.

The only thing left was sweet-talking her.

Almost at the door, Seth turned. "If you don't mind, I think I'll run this pregnancy by George Green."

Jake's brow furrowed. "The private investigator?"

"You dated Avery Novak for only three weeks, but you don't think you need a DNA test. You don't seem to care that she's moving to Pennsylvania. Either you're still half in love with her—"

"I'm not."

"Or you're so happy to be having a child you're not thinking clearly."

He sighed. "I'm thinking perfectly fine."

"Let me call George anyway, have him do a bit of research into her past to make sure everything's okay."

"I don't know."

"It's just a precaution. Plus, you never know what he'll find. Maybe there's something in her past that could help you."

Jake ran his hand across his mouth. Calling a private investigator to make sure Avery was on the up-and-up was one thing. But digging up dirt, ruining someone's life to extort them into compliance sounded so much like something his father would do after one of his fits of rage that he hesitated.

"Look, Jake, Mom's already at odds. If this blows up in your face, she's going to go over the edge. You know it. I know it. This isn't just about you."

Jake tossed his pencil to his desk. "All right. Call George. But I want to be the one to talk to him."

"Great. I'll set a meeting for this afternoon."

"Not at the office."

"Your place?"

He hesitated again. A horrible feeling washed through him. Was he pulling one of his dad's tricks? Looking for something in Avery's past? His intention was to make sure Avery could be trusted, but what if he found something that might make her seem unfit? Would he take her baby?

He stopped himself. There was no reason to get ahead of himself. A woman he barely knew, albeit that she'd been vetted by Waters, Waters and Montgomery when they'd hired her, was having his child. There was nothing wrong with checking up on her. Plus, he couldn't dismiss what Seth was saying. Their mom was fragile. Their father might have been dead five months, but she wasn't bouncing back from the loss. They didn't need a scandal, or worse yet, a thief in their lives right now.

"Have him meet me at my house at about six."

The feeling rolled through him again. The awful fear that he was becoming his dad. This time, he ignored it.

* * *

As Avery arrived at her office, she closed the door and hit the Contacts button on her phone to call her mom.

She hadn't been able to sleep the night before. After hours of tossing and turning, she'd realized she'd been lulled into a false sense that she was in control of this situation with Jake because she had a Plan A, Plan B and even Plan C.

But Jake McCallan was much too careful, too smart. Sleeping with her ten times had been one thing. Having her as the mother of his child was quite another. If he hadn't checked into her past before this, he would be checking now.

And once he did, Plan C would be as dead in the water as Plan A, and Plan B wouldn't stand a chance.

Still, right now, her priority was to warn her mom.

When she answered, Avery said, "Hey, Mom."

"Avery! What a nice surprise. What's up? You never call on a weekday."

She winced. She didn't like reopening old wounds, but she wouldn't let her mom be blindsided. "I have a feeling some people are going to be coming around asking questions about me."

"You mean like the private investigators who checked into your life when you were hired by the big law firm?"

Avery said, "Yes," but her heart stuttered. Pregnancy hormones must be making her slow and dull. Jake wouldn't have to hire a private investigator to check out her past. All he had to do was ask her boss. Pete Waters had investigated her before he hired her. But where Waters, Waters and Montgomery considered it an advantage to employ a woman whose dad had been unjustly convicted—because it motivated her to work hard for their clients— all Jake would see was that her dad had been in jail.

And he could use that.

She ran her hand through her hair and walked to the filing cabinet. There were no windows in her office. Associates didn't get offices with windows. That was her place. A very small person in a very big world. A world that was quickly spinning out of control.

She squeezed her eyes shut. There was absolutely no way to fight this. "This is a mess, Mom. It's going to bring up all Dad's troubles again for you guys."

"Avery," her mom said softly. "We live it every day. The whole town knows your dad was in jail but got out when Project Freedom proved he'd been framed. Let someone come and ask questions. We're fine."

"Okay."

"But that doesn't mean we don't want you starting your law firm. Your dad went through hell for six years and we don't want to see that happen to anybody else."

"Neither do I."

"And we're proud of you."

"Thanks." She sucked in a breath, blew it out slowly. Her parents being okay with an investigator coming to town solved one problem. But there were thirty others nipping at her heels, things she wouldn't burden her mom with.

"So…this guy who's coming to ask us questions…does this have anything to do with the baby?"

She swallowed. She should have known her mom would figure this out. Who else from New York would care about her dad's past?

"The baby's father and I ran into each other. He saw I was pregnant and pretty much did the math."

"And you think he's going to look into your past hoping to find something he can use to get custody of the baby?"

"He might. Or he might just use it to keep me in New York."

"Oh."

Her mother's hopeless tone caused all of Avery's fears to rush to the surface. "He could ruin all my plans."

"Or maybe the two of you could work this out?"

The more she thought about it, the more she doubted it. But to placate her mom she said, "Sure."

"I mean it." Her mother's voice brightened. "All you need is a little trust. In fact, if you told him about your dad so he didn't have to send a private investigator to Wilton, then he might see you're an honest person and negotiate a little more fairly."

Avery laughed. "That is the most optimistic thing I've ever heard."

"Sweetie, he's going to find out anyway. And if you don't tell him, it might make him suspicious and maybe even angry that you held such important information back. But if you tell him, it could be your door of opportunity to start some trust between you."

Her mother sounded so sure that for a second Avery waivered. "I don't know."

"Your dad and I aren't running. You shouldn't either. Face this head-on."

If it was anybody else but Jake McCallan, she might be able to cobble together enough optimism to give it a shot. Knowing her mother would keep trying to persuade her if she didn't at least say she'd consider it, Avery said, "I'll think about it."

After some gossip about the flower shop owner, Avery hung up the phone and squeezed her eyes shut. If Jake discovered her father's past and confronted her, she could come out swinging, quote bits and pieces from the hearings that freed him and defend him.

But to tell Jake herself? To explain that her dad had been framed by a coworker with a sick wife, who could have freed him the day his wife died but waited until his own death to admit to his crime? To tell Jake about weeks and months of waiting for hearings, about having her dad's old boss oppose a new trial, about the worry that Paul Barnes had bribed the judge? It would be one of the most vulnerable moments of her life. She was a fighter, not a beggar.

But her mother was right. Jake was going to find out. And soon. If she could humble herself to explain this to him, it *might* be the beginning of trust between them.

Then maybe she could use Plan C. Once she told him about her dad, reminding him of the field day the media would have could show him how difficult having her baby in his life would be.

It was risky. But as her mom had said, he was going to find out anyway.

She got to work to take her mind off everything. An hour later, her private cell phone rang. She glanced down, saw the caller was Jake and squeezed her eyes shut before she answered.

"Good morning, Jake."

"I'd like to finish our discussion from last night. How about dinner tonight at 4 Charles Prime Rib?"

She blew her breath out in a quiet stream. She didn't want to cause an argument, but if she was going to tell him about her dad, she didn't want to go to a restaurant. Especially not some place where anyone could see them and where paparazzi hung out at the entry, waiting for celebrities. One look at the pregnant belly on Jake's date and the photographers would go nuts taking pictures.

"Maybe a coffee shop would be better? Someplace low-key."

A few seconds passed in silence. He clearly wasn't thrilled to have her change his plan.

"I just don't want to run into the photographers who hang out in front of those ritzy restaurants you like."

He sighed. "Okay. How about that small coffee shop up the street from your condo?"

"Great. That would be great."

She hung up the phone equal parts grateful for the opportunity to talk to him and terrified at the thousands of ways this discussion could go wrong.

At nine o'clock, she strode up the still busy street to the brick building housing the coffee shop where she was meeting Jake. Large windows fronted the well-lit establishment. The place was crowded with chatting people hovering at the bar on the left, or lounging at one of the curved booths with cushioned seats.

She stepped inside, glanced around and found Jake in the back, at one of the compact wooden tables for two. Disciplined Jake wouldn't waste the space of one of the big comfy booths, no matter how much she would have loved to sink her tired body into those cushions right now.

Convinced her mother was right—with the addition of Plan C—and ready to have the discussion, she walked up to the table. "Hi."

He rose. Nice-fitting trousers and a pale blue dress shirt outlined muscles created in the gym. Her mouth all but watered. But she told herself to settle down. Not to salivate over how good-looking he was, or to realize how easily she could unbutton that shirt and feel all the fabulous muscles of his chest.

Her breath shivered and she took a quiet drink of air to steady herself. "I see you went home to change."

"I had some time."

Something about the way he said that set her warning signals to high alert. But before she could say anything, he asked, "Can I get you a coffee?"

She shook her head. "I'll have a bottle of water. I can't drink coffee. Another unfortunate side effect of pregnancy."

"Another?"

She sure as hell wasn't going to tell him that pregnant women were easily aroused or that just looking at him had made her want to rip his shirt off. "You'd be surprised what happens to a body when a woman is pregnant."

He walked away and she settled herself on the seat across from his while he went for her water.

Setting it on the table in front of her, he asked, "So did you have morning sickness?"

She opened the bottle. "Horribly."

"But that only lasts the first trimester, right?"

He'd done some homework. More proof that if he didn't already know about her dad, he would soon.

"Yes. But some things bring it back."

"Like what things?"

"You're going to laugh, but certain tooth-pastes just about kill me."

He caught her gaze as he sat across from her. "Really?"

"I went through four brands before I found something I could brush my teeth with."

He laughed.

She rolled her eyes. "Consider yourself very, very lucky that your part in creating this baby was a lot more pleasant."

He laughed again and Avery said a silent prayer for strength. She'd never seen him this comfortable or relaxed. There might never be another chance as perfect as this to tell him her father's story.

She sat up straighter, pulling together all her confidence—

"Why if it isn't the lovely and talented Jake McCallan."

Avery's head snapped to the right and she saw the pretty blonde who'd walked up to their table.

Jake groaned. "What do you want, Sabrina?"

The blonde smiled at Jake. "Nothing." She slid a glance at Avery. "I just rarely see you anywhere but the office and dinner once a week at Mom's. And with company too."

Jake shook his head. "Avery, this is my sister, Sabrina. Sabrina, this is Avery Novak. She works at Waters, Waters and Montgomery."

Sabrina extended her hand.

Avery froze. *His sister* just happened to be in the same coffee shop where they'd planned to meet twelve hours ago?

Shell-shocked and confused, she took the hand Sabrina extended. Social convention dictated that she rise, but then she'd expose the baby bump. And it wouldn't be long before everyone in his family would know she was pregnant. And once the news was out, it would really be "out." They'd tell their friends. Everyone would know. There'd be no way to ease him out of the picture. No way for him to quietly disassociate himself from her.

Damn. She had no idea why she thought she could trust him. The minute he was out of her sight, he'd probably told his entire family. Worse, he hadn't warned her that he'd told them. How could she explain her dad's situation to him and think he'd listen? Think he'd keep it to himself and give her what she wanted? He wouldn't. Let it come out in court, at a custody battle, where the evidence could speak for itself.

Or maybe it wouldn't.

Maybe his lawyers would twist it the way

Paul Barnes had gotten the DA to twist the evidence of her father's innocence into a story of a coworker who'd only confessed after he was dead to get his friend out of prison.

Damn it! Damn it! Damn it!

She couldn't deal with this right now. Especially not in front of his sister.

She popped out of her seat, grabbed her purse and turned away from the table. "We'll talk another time, Jake."

Her pulse pounding, she raced out the door and into the hot first-day-of-September evening. She couldn't believe how this situation kept spiraling. Anger poured through her in waves. If she couldn't trust Jake not to say anything to anyone until they had their situation resolved, how could she trust him with anything?

A hand caught her arm, slowed her down, then stopped her.

It had to be Jake.

She spun to face him. "Now what? Would you like me to sit with a reporter from the *New Yorker* and give an interview? Maybe we can get ABC to put us on *Good Morning America*?"

"Will you stop? I didn't tell her to come here!"

"You expect me to believe it was a coincidence?"

"It *was*! And you're being stupid. It was my sister for God's sake. Not a girlfriend."

"I would have much rather that she'd been a girlfriend!"

He stepped close. "Really?"

He smelled spicy and male and all her pregnancy hormones popped. She ignored them. "You can date anybody you want."

"I'm about to be a father. I want to settle one life crisis at a time. I don't want to date anybody."

"Well, you might as well, because you and I are oil and water. Our lives clash. Even when we try to get along, we fight. We'll never get a custody agreement hammered out. We're going to end up in court."

"Because you intend to be stubborn?"

"Because I had a *plan*!" Three plans, actually. And all three had failed. "You don't believe this about me, but I love plans. I love order. Just because I don't say it with a calm, rational voice, doesn't mean I—"

He caught her by the upper arms and hauled her against him, and for twenty seconds they stared into each other's eyes. Warmth coursed through her. Her breasts met his chest. Their baby bumped against his stomach.

A million emotions flashed through his blue eyes. She was pretty sure his intention had been to stop her tirade by kissing her. Then he'd felt the baby bump and frozen.

Except for those eyes. Every emotion from confusion to fear to happy surprise and anger raced through them.

CHAPTER THREE

JAKE DROPPED HER ARMS then stepped back, away from the temptation of Avery's mouth.

He couldn't believe how desperately he wanted to kiss her. He'd caught her arms to shut her up, but staring into her eyes he'd remembered her fire and wanted to taste it again. Then he'd felt the baby—*his baby*—and his brain had scattered in a million directions.

"Well, that was interesting."

"Not really." She shrugged. "You said yourself we both prolonged our relationship because we were so hot in bed. We're accustomed to touching each other. And when we touch, sparks fly."

"That's about the size of it." He took another step back. Not wanting to talk about the myriad feelings racing through him when he'd felt the baby bump, he said, "It really was a coincidence that we ran into Sabrina."

She took a breath, then looked away as if

thinking it through. Her long red hair shimmered when her head moved, and he struggled not to reach out and touch it. Not to reach out and touch *her*, if only in amazement that she carried his child. But that was wrong. A weakness he couldn't afford with her.

When she caught his gaze, the anger was gone from her eyes too.

"We're both just a little too edgy right now. Not sure of each other or how to handle this situation. We're going to have to be more careful about where we meet next time."

"Should we meet in one of our apartments?"

"No. We should meet in *mine*. We never know who's lurking in the bushes outside yours. And—" She held his gaze with an intensity that might have scared another man but almost made him laugh. He had no doubt why Pete Waters considered her his top associate. That stare could terrify any witness and probably some judges.

"No more touching on public streets." She looked around then glanced back at him again. "We don't know who could have seen that."

He said, "Sure," as she turned and walked away. The way she could so easily leave, snatching control out of his hands again, sent a wave of annoyance through him. "I notice you didn't say anything about touching on private streets. Maybe alleyways. The lobby of your building."

She didn't turn around, didn't acknowledge anything he'd said, just kept striding up the street.

A laugh escaped. She might not have turned, but she'd heard him. He'd seen the way her spine straightened. God help him, but he'd needed the validation that he still got to her, still had a little bit of control. Even if it was only teasing her.

When he pivoted to return to the coffee shop, he almost plowed into his sister.

"Mom is going to have a cow."

All the fun of teasing Avery instantly evaporated.

Sabrina's face fell. "You are going to tell her, aren't you?"

"Eventually."

"Eventually? That woman has got to be at least six months pregnant! What are you going to do? Call Mom from the hospital and say, *It's a boy*?"

"I'd like a boy." He really would. Someone to teach everything he knew. Someone to inherit everything he'd worked for. Now that he was adjusting to being a dad, the thought filled him with a pleasure that was almost indescribable. If he and Avery weren't the worst possible match, he might think this was fate. Destiny. A sign they were meant to be together.

Of course, though it might not be romantic fate, it still could be fate. Not a way to bring him and Avery together, but a way for him to have an heir.

"Are you even listening to anything I said!"

Forcing himself back to reality, he sighed. "Yes. I heard you. You think I should tell Mom."

"Soon."

"All right. Soon."

But the more he thought about fate and heirs, the more he realized that he'd have to see Pete Waters again—at the corporate headquarters. Not Pete's office. Avery Novak wasn't just smart. She was sexy and unpredictable. And he'd already slipped and almost kissed her. He had to get the facts about his parental rights before he tangled with her again.

But he didn't get the chance to summon Pete to his office. The first thing the next morning, his phone blew up with calls from his lawyer. There were thirteen messages that started at five, while Jake was in the shower, and kept going until Jake finally walked into his room and saw his phone blinking hysterically, as if Pete had continually hit Redial.

When the phone rang again, he answered.

Pete didn't even bother with hello. "Are you crazy?"

"I think we both know I'm not."

"Then why is there a picture of you with Avery Novak in the society pages?" Pete's voice rose. "Are you the father of Avery's baby?"

Jake squeezed his eyes shut. "Yes."

"Hell. When she told me she was pregnant, she said she had no intention of marrying her baby's father. And she's returning to Pennsylvania after the baby's born."

"Her leaving New York doesn't have to be a big deal."

"It will be to your mother!"

He knew that. But right now, he was more concerned with the picture of himself and pregnant Avery in the newspaper. He didn't want his mom to see it and have a meltdown, especially when this was an easy fix.

"Okay. I'll fly to Paris today instead of tomorrow and tell her." He paused for a second to consider, but only a second. Avery was responsible for most of this mess. He wasn't flying to Paris alone. "And consider this Avery's official call that she's taking the rest of the week off."

"She can take the next month off because there's no way in hell I can let her touch anything that even remotely relates to any of your cases. You do realize at some point you'll be on opposite ends of a custody battle? The conflict of interest is off the charts if she even touches a file that relates to you or your family or your company."

"I know that. But you have to give me a minute to catch my breath, Pete. She only told me on Monday. I'm just starting to wrap my head around the ramifications of all this. What I need from you right now is a summary of my rights and choices."

"This is something I'd usually hand off to Avery." He sighed deeply. "This is a mess."

"It doesn't have to be. We all just have to keep our heads and handle it."

Pete sighed again. "I'll assign someone to write your summary."

"Good."

"It'll be waiting when you get back."

"Email it to me."

Jake hung up and phoned his driver then dressed quickly, but not in a suit. He pulled on casual pants and a sports shirt and covered them with a navy blue blazer. When he reached the street, the limo awaited him. Twenty minutes later, he was knocking on Avery's door.

Wearing black slacks and a pretty peach-colored blouse that highlighted her long red hair, she opened the door.

When she saw him, she groaned. "If whatever you want takes more than two minutes, I'm going to be late for work."

As she stepped back, he walked into her condo. "You don't have to go to work today. Remember how you worried someone would see us yesterday?"

She crossed her arms on her chest.

"You were right. A reporter for the *Gazette* took a picture. We made the society pages. Baby bump and all."

"Oh, no." She sank onto one of her club chairs.

"My mother's in Paris and I had planned on flying there for the weekend, but I told Pete we'd go today and tell my mom before she sees it online."

She gaped at him. "You told my boss my baby is yours?"

"No. *My lawyer* saw the picture in the paper. He figured it out and called me."

"And he's sending me to Paris with you?"

"No. Having you go was my idea."

She bounced out of the chair and grabbed her briefcase. "Then I'm not going! I have a job."

He winced. "Well, you do but you're off anything that has to do with McCallan, Inc."

Her face fell. The briefcase slid to the floor. "Pete says it's conflict of interest since we could be on opposing sides of a custody battle."

"There are still plenty of other things for me to work on. The firm has defense cases that don't even nip the edge of any of your corporate work. Those are the ones I want anyway."

"That's for you and Pete to settle when we get back. Right now, we have to tell my mother about the baby. And before you argue, I'm not doing this alone. *You* kept this from me for six months. I'm sure you had your reasons. But the bottom line is, we are both this baby's parents. If we want to make fair, equitable decisions for our child, that starts with us presenting a unified front right from the beginning."

Avery stared at him for a few seconds. Though she wanted to argue, she saw his point. They did need to start being parents to their child. And she suddenly saw what her mom was talking about when she said they needed a step to begin trusting each other. If she did this for him now, that could begin a trend of cooperation.

Or maybe this could be the first step of their negotiations?

"I want to strike a deal."

His eyes narrowed. "A deal?"

"I'll go to Paris with you, if you agree not to use something in my dad's past against me when we start talking custody."

"Something your *father* did?"

"Do we have a deal or not?"

"Was he a serial killer?"

"Actually, he didn't do anything wrong." She winced. "That's kind of the point."

"He didn't do anything wrong, but people thought he did."

"Yes."

"So, he was unjustly accused of something."

"He was actually tried and convicted. He spent six years in prison. Then one of his co-workers confessed that he'd framed my dad. He also produced sufficient evidence that my father was innocent and eventually he was released."

"Oh."

She pointed at her watch. "Time is ticking away. If you don't want the deal I need to go to work. My father is as innocent as a newborn baby. One of the nicest guys you would ever meet. It wouldn't be fair for you to dredge it all up again. Worse, if you did, it would reflect poorly on you."

"Yes. It would." His head tilted. An odd expression flitted across his face. "So, the deal is you'll go to Paris with me if I don't bring up what happened to your dad."

"Yes."

"Okay."

Relief washed through her. It wasn't exactly the culmination of any of her plans, but she'd won a significant victory.

"Good. Let me pack a few things and we can be on our way."

She tossed a dress and enough jeans and T-shirts, undies and toiletries for a day or two into her scuffed-up duffel bag. As she slid the wide strap to her shoulder, she caught a glimpse of her reflection and grimaced. The thing looked as if it had gone through a war. Just like most of her personal possessions. She might live in a beautiful home in a great part of the city, but only because her condo had been an investment. When she returned to Pennsylvania, she would live in a small house in a small town. Most of her money would go toward her practice.

She'd always have enough to take good care of her child but he or she certainly wouldn't live in the lap of luxury. Her condo and nice work clothes might have fooled Jake into thinking she had more than she did, but she wouldn't be able to hide the truth forever. She was squarely in the middle class.

Her relief at her deal with Jake faded into nothing. Getting him to agree not to use her dad was a victory, but there were so many other things he could use. So many other ways he could keep her in New York, destroying the goal she'd been working toward since she was a teenager. Especially since she'd planned on her child going to public school, taking a bag lunch and riding the bus. None of this would sit well with the clan McCallan.

Jake had tons of things he could use about her life, about what she wanted to do with her life, to give him leverage.

She and Jake took the elevator to the lobby and walked onto the street. At six thirty, the city was beginning to show signs of life. Car tires made soft swishing noises as they drove through puddles left behind by the storm the night before. Streetlights flickered as the sky shifted to whitish gray.

Jake directed her to a black limo. The driver opened the door and she slid inside onto white leather seats. Jake slid in behind her.

The driver closed the door and Avery heard another door open and shut. The engine started. The limo began to move.

Jake smiled ruefully. "I rushed you so much. I'm not even sure you've had coffee yet."

"Can't have coffee, remember?" She glanced

around, her tension mounting. A family accustomed to limos would not let their first grandchild ride a big yellow school bus.

He winced. "Sorry. I've got some juice stocked if you'd like that."

She nodded. "Yes. Apple if you have it."

He opened the door of what looked like a console table exposing three bottles of juice. All of them orange.

"You sure you don't want orange juice?"

"It gives me heartburn."

"Sorry. We can stop somewhere."

"No. I'm fine. Let's just get to the airport."

Pulling his phone from his pants pocket, he said, "We're not going to the airport. We use a private airstrip." He hit a speed dial number. "And everything you need will be on the plane."

The person he'd called must have answered because he said, "Andre? I need you to make sure there's apple juice on the plane. And…" He caught her gaze. "Eggs for breakfast? Oatmeal? Box cereal? Bacon?"

Bacon? Her stomach growled. There was no sense in pretending she wasn't hungry. "Bacon and eggs and rye toast would be great."

"With apple juice?"

"With apple juice."

They reached the airstrip in just a bit over an hour, and climbed onto the McCallan family's private jet. She'd expected something compact and simple. Instead, she entered luxury so intense it magnified all her fears. The setup of the front space was more like a den than an airplane cabin.

Jake pointed to a door in the back of that section. "The kitchen is behind the first door and behind that are two small bedrooms." He pressed a button and the cabinet doors eased apart to reveal a large-screen TV. "And that's the TV."

She swallowed. They hadn't dated long enough for her to meet his mother or fly in his jet. His apartment and assortment of limos and drivers had been enough to scare her. Seeing the rest of his lifestyle sent another shock wave of reality through her.

If she thought she could control this situation with Jake, get him to visit their child in Pennsylvania, never bring her to his own home, in his jet or to the family's three-story penthouse across from Central Park, she'd only been kidding herself.

And she was in way over her head.

CHAPTER FOUR

FOG PREVENTED THEM from leaving until nine. The cook made good use of the time by preparing breakfast and some sandwiches for lunch before he headed back to the city.

Jake watched in amusement as Avery ate like a starving woman. But he didn't say anything. He was getting smarter about dealing with her. Negotiating had worked to get her to go to Paris with him to tell his mother about the baby. Though there was no way he'd have used her dad's conviction against her—particularly since her father had been exonerated—finally having her tell him something personal was a significant first step.

So maybe they could use the eight-hour flight to talk some more, open some doors, make some more deals?

He settled in on the comfortable sofa, close enough to Avery that they could talk but not so close that he'd spook her. He'd be light, congenial, maybe get her to chat a little more about her dad so he could tell her he didn't want to ride roughshod over her, just see his child. And they could figure this out.

But as soon as the fasten seatbelts light went out, Avery opened her briefcase.

"What are you doing?"

She glanced over at him, her stunning green eyes cautious. "Taking a few days off means I'll fall behind. I can't afford to fall behind."

"If what I'm guessing about conflict of interest is true, your caseload just got a lot smaller. A few days off won't matter. Why don't you relax?"

"Because I need this job for another three months. I want to be able to show Pete he can still count on me. I'll rest after the baby's born."

"I think you're crazy. You should take advantage of the unexpected free time."

She set her file on her lap. "Are you telling me you aren't going to work at all in this very long flight?"

"I'm not." But he should. Except he hadn't thought to bring his briefcase. Even panicked about his mother, he should have remembered this nearly eight-hour flight and been prepared. But adrenaline over seeing Avery and coaxing her to go to Paris with him had pushed his job out of his head.

He couldn't recall ever forgetting something so important because of a woman and peeked over at her. She'd removed her black blazer. The peachy color of her blouse enhanced the red of her hair. Her complexion glowed. She *was* gorgeous. And soft. Her pale, pale skin was probably the softest he'd ever touched.

The memory of it stirred his blood, scrambled his pulse.

So maybe he wasn't in the best frame of mind to negotiate visitation?

He cleared his throat. "What are you working on?"

She didn't even look up. "Haven't you ever heard of client confidentiality?"

He shrugged. "I am your client."

"You're not *this* client."

She fixed her attention on the papers in the file. Bored and deciding that watching the news was better than staring at the top of Avery's head, Jake turned on the TV.

She glared at him. "Seriously. I'm trying to focus here. I'm sure there's a television in one of those bedrooms of yours back there."

There was. But he didn't really want to watch anything. He wanted to talk to her. Even if he was a bit confused by her right now, he needed to figure this out. He didn't like things hanging in the air. He wanted this solved.

An antsy sensation snaked along his skin. A memory of something his dad used to say. *Desperate people make mistakes. Never go into a negotiation desperate.*

He sucked in a breath. If there was anything he hated worse than fearing he was like his father, it was realizing something his father said was actually true. The pregnancy *had* rattled him. Becoming a dad was equal parts frightening and exciting. The mother of his child was too different to second-guess her motives or plans. She was also gorgeous. And thinking about all that wasn't helping.

He glanced at her briefcase and saw her silent laptop. He pointed at it. "Can I use that?"

She peered up again. "My laptop?"

"Yes."

"You didn't bring anything to do, did you?"

He sighed. "No. Foolishly, I thought we'd talk, remember?"

"I'm working."

"So you've said."

She took the laptop from her briefcase, opened it and started typing.

"Don't pretend you need it just because I want to use it."

She didn't even look up. "I'm not pretending I need it. I'm creating a screen name for you, so you don't have to use mine and won't be able to see any of my documents."

"I'm not interested in your documents."

"You already asked about the case I'm working on. I don't want to take a chance that your curiosity will get the better of you."

"I'm not curious."

Her fingers click, click, clicked across the keyboard. "I think you are."

He gaped at her. How did she do that? Twist what he said and did into a completely wrong meaning? He swore sometimes she did it on purpose.

Or maybe she didn't have any other frame of reference?

He knew very little about her background. She knew very little about his. Because they hadn't really talked when they met up those ten times. They'd had better things to do.

She handed him the laptop.

"Thank you."

"You're welcome." She turned her attention to her file again. "I'm guessing you have off-site storage and you can get into your files."

"Yes."

"Good."

Her tone said she was already out of the conversation, but he still studied her. Realizing they fought because they didn't understand each other wasn't a great leap. The question was, did he want to do anything about it? He'd planned to negotiate with her, but if she refused to talk, the courts—and his superstar lawyers—would get him a good deal.

Maybe he should just let it all alone? Let her work and ignore him. While he worked and ignored her. Stop trying to be friends?

That suddenly seemed like a very good idea.

He accessed his files and got lost in the financials for a project that was going sour, relaxing in the world he knew. Money. How to make it work for him. How to make sure his family never ran out. How to assure the Mc-Callan legacy stood forever. The family name lived forever. Because that's what he did. He made plans. He took control. And sometimes that control came in the form of letting his lawyers handle things.

Four hours later, they ate the sandwiches that had been prepared by the cook. Then Avery took a nap that lasted until an hour before they landed. When she woke, she spent the rest of the flight finishing up the work she'd been doing that morning. When the pilot turned on the fasten seatbelts sign, she tucked her files and notepads into her briefcase, then collected the laptop she'd lent him.

While she all but ignored him, he focused

on deciding what he would say to his mom, introducing Avery to her and—hopefully— avoiding a meltdown.

Because at this point, that's where his priority lay. With fixing that part of this problem.

Their descent into Paris was silent. Avery knew Jake was a bit miffed at her for not talking, but she was fine with that. She wasn't sticking her foot in her mouth or saying something she'd regret by speaking before she was ready. Especially since the consequences of his finding out about their baby were finally sinking in.

Number one, she would lose her job. Conflict of interest wasn't simply a matter of her not working on any of his cases. She couldn't work for the law firm representing Jake in their custody battle. Not just for Jake's protection, but for hers.

Number two, they would go to court over visitation. Jake was accustomed to getting his own way and would make demands she could never agree to. A judge would have to decide.

Number three, she needed an attorney. Hearings were no problem for Jake. He had a battery of lawyers, while she had…herself. She could probably do a credible job on her own, but someone once said a man who acts as his own attorney has a fool for a client. She wasn't losing her dream of starting her law firm in Pennsylvania, or losing control of her child's life because she didn't spend the money for good counsel. As soon as she got back to New York, she would hire a lawyer.

Figuring all that out restored her confidence. The jet landed at eleven o'clock at night Paris time, though it was only five o'clock in New York. Walking to a waiting limo, Avery watched workers scurry to get their bags from the belly of the plane. In ten minutes, they were on the road.

"So how long until we get to the hotel?"

"Forty minutes."

Still gruff. Still miffed.

Which was fine, except his gruffness reminded her of dating him, and that reminded her of stealing time at his penthouse, making love in his shower, grabbing a bagel on the way out the door because they didn't stop to talk.

Neither of them had wanted to.

She ended those thoughts by looking out the window, at the countryside rolling by. It was too dark to see anything except open fields that gave way to clusters of houses and eventually the city.

Avery's senses perked up. She'd never been to Europe before, let alone Paris. *The* Paris. Not just city of love, but city of culture and history. And, oh, dear God, the architecture. Streetlights showcased aged brick-and-stone buildings that lined the avenues like society matrons in the receiving line of an ambassador's ball. The Eiffel Tower was lit like a beacon. Moonlight sparkled off the Seine.

By the time they reached their hotel, she was breathless. The limo pulled up in front of the entry of a building that looked to be five or six stories. White columns and white shutters accented weathered red brick. Brass lamps sat on either side of a revolving door trimmed in the same shiny metal.

The rotating door guided them into the lobby, as Jake walked with her, his hand on her elbow guiding her.

Which was probably more necessary than she wanted to admit. Her head swiveled from side to side, as she took in the luxurious black, gold and white lobby. She would have run into the bellman, two other hotel patrons and a coffee table if he hadn't steered her away.

The man behind the reservation desk nodded to him. In perfect English, he said, "Good evening, Mr. McCallan." He nodded at Avery. "Mademoiselle."

"Good evening."

"Your room, of course, is ready." He handed a key card to Jake. "It's your favorite."

"Thank you." He pocketed the key. "Have the concierge call the Bristol. Let my mother know we've arrived safely."

"Very good."

Avery's happy bubble burst. She'd forgotten they were in Paris to talk to his mom. Working during the flight, thinking through her ever-changing situation with Jake and ogling the architecture on the drive here, she hadn't given herself twenty seconds to prepare.

She glanced around the lush, expensive lobby, which suddenly seemed like a symbol for Jake's mom. Fancy, elegant, rich.

She was so out of her element that hiring an attorney now looked like the smartest conclusion she'd ever drawn. She could not handle this family, fight their money, on her own, any more than her dad could fight Paul Barnes with a public defender.

They rode up in the elevator in silence and walked down an equally quiet corridor. White-wood-trimmed walls were painted a soothing gray. When Jake opened the door on the last room on the right, she realized she was following him to *one* room. *His* room.

"Are we sharing a room?"

"It's a suite."

It was a gorgeous suite. The original features of wide wood trim and carved crown molding paired with thick throw rugs and a comfortable sofa and chair to create a sitting room that was both sophisticated and comfortable.

"I'm not sleeping with you."

"I never asked you to."

"Why not just get me my own room?"

"Because I don't want you to be alone."

"What you really mean is you're afraid I'll bolt and you'll be on your own with your mother."

"No. Because if you bolt our deal is off. And that's not good for you." He sighed. "Look, you're a pregnant woman in a strange city. Do you speak French?"

Her chin lifted. "Do you?"

He rattled off a line as smooth as silk and deliciously sexy.

"Point taken."

"So, we settle in, have dinner and get a good night's sleep before we talk to my mom in the morning. If we're lucky, you'll be back on the jet noon tomorrow."

Disappointment sneaked up on her before she could stop it. She probably didn't have a job to go back to. And she was in Paris. *Paris*. They were going to eat in a hotel, sleep, see his mom, then fly out? It hardly seemed fair.

The bellman discreetly entered. Jake pointed to the right. "Ms. Novak will take that room."

He turned and pointed at the second door. "I'll take that room."

As the bellman distributed their bags, Jake shrugged out of his jacket. "Before I shower, I'll order room service. By the time I'm out, our dinner should be here."

She sighed. "All neat and tidy, huh?"

"I'm tired, I'm hungry and tomorrow I have to tell my mom she's going to be a grandmother in a few months, but we never told her. I'll have to explain why she missed the joy of knowing, of seeing your belly grow, of buying gifts and telling her friends. If I want to relax in the shower I don't think that's too much to ask."

Unexpected guilt shimmied through her. She'd never thought of his mother missing out. Mostly because she'd just plain never thought of his mother, never added her into the equation of the pregnancy.

She remembered her own mother's elation when Avery had told her. And her dad's—

Jake's dad died without knowing he would be a grandfather.

Sorrow swooped through her heart, leaving a trail of gut-wrenching regret in its wake. "I'm so sorry."

Halfway to his room, he faced her. "You're sorry?"

"Yes."

His expression shifted, softened. "I think that's the first time I've ever heard you say that." Then he turned and walked into his room.

She fell to the sofa. Guilt sat on her shoulders like one of the gargoyles she'd seen on a nearby building. She squeezed her eyes shut, then rose from the sofa and headed to her room.

Trying not to think about any of that, she showered. But as she stood in front of the mirror drying, she saw her pregnant belly.

She put her hands on either side just as the baby kicked. She hadn't merely deprived Jake's parents of the gift of knowing they were to be grandparents. She'd deprived Jake of so much more.

She slid the shower cap off her long, unruly red hair and combed it out before slipping into panties, a bra and an oversize T-shirt, getting ready for bed. She added the thick white robe provided by the hotel because the room had a slight chill. Then she padded to the door and opened it.

He was right about the food. A table had been set in the middle of the room, complete with a white linen cloth and a lovely bouquet of flowers as a centerpiece.

Jake stood by the window, looking out at the stunning display of lights woven through the city. When her door closed with a soft click, he turned from the window.

He wore sweatpants and a T-shirt, something similar to what he'd worn in the mornings when she'd stayed over at his penthouse. A memory tiptoed through her again. Him giving her a sexy kiss goodbye before she raced away to catch an elevator.

"I never thought to ask if you were hungry."

The aroma of beef hit her, bringing her back to the present. She closed her eyes to savor it. "Starved."

"I took the liberty of ordering a steak for both of us, but there's also a bowl of steamed vegetables, and macaroni and cheese."

"Macaroni and cheese and steak?"

"If it's too fattening, eat one or the other."

She approached the table. "Are you kidding? It's my dream meal."

He headed for the table, too. "Good."

Before she could pull out her chair, he reached for it.

"Thank you."

"You're welcome."

He sat across from her and lifted the silver warmer from his plate. "Both steaks are medium."

She lifted her warmer, too, and let the scent drift out to her. "Smells perfect."

"Bread?"

He handed the basket to her and she winced. "I think steak and macaroni are enough calories for one night."

He laughed. Sort of. He clearly thought what she'd said was funny, but he wasn't ready to fully laugh with her yet. She supposed she didn't blame him.

"So, have you figured out what to say to your mother?"

He shrugged. "Yes and no. I have a few ideas of how to soften the blow because I know how surprised she'll be, and the loss she'll feel when she realizes how much she missed."

Because he'd felt it too. He didn't have to say the words, she could hear the regret in his voice. Guilt rippled through her again at the same time the baby kicked.

She set down her fork and rose from her seat. She couldn't make up for what he'd missed before—mostly morning sickness and exhaustion so she couldn't feel too much remorse—but she could bring him up to speed right now.

Walking to his side of the table, she undid the belt of the fluffy white robe. "Baby's kicking. Want to feel?"

CHAPTER FIVE

H IS GAZE FLEW to hers, his eyes wide with surprise. "Really?"

"Sure."

Her T-shirt was so long she didn't worry about the fact that she wore only bra and panties beneath it. The robe fell open.

He looked at her belly.

"Go ahead. Lay your hands on either side."

He gingerly laid one hand on her T-shirt-covered baby bump.

She reached down and took his other hand and brought it to her stomach too. "We may have to wait a few seconds…oops. No. There he is." She laughed. "Or she."

Jake laughed nervously. "Oh, my goodness."

"Feeling that makes it real, doesn't it?"

"Yes."

His voice was hoarse, so soft that she barely heard him. They had a mere three weeks of dating, but she knew that tone. His voice had gotten that way only one other time—the first time he'd seen her naked.

Something inside her cracked just a little bit. Her pride. He might be a stuffy aristocrat, but there was a part of him that was a normal man. And though she had her reasons for not wanting him to be involved with her child, she had to play fair.

The baby kicked again, and she stayed right where she was. "Ask me anything. I can see you're dying to know."

He smoothed his hands along her T-shirt as if memorizing the shape of her belly. "I'm not even sure what to ask."

"There's not a lot to tell. You already know I had morning sickness. At the end of a long day, I'm usually exhausted. But as far as the baby is concerned, this—" she motioned to her tummy "—feeling him move—is as good as it gets."

The baby stopped. She waited a few seconds to see if he'd start up again, but he didn't.

She stepped back. "Food's getting cold."

"Yes. Of course. Please eat."

She smiled slightly and retied the belt of her robe as she walked back to her seat.

After spooning some macaroni and cheese into one of the small bowls provided, she dug in with gusto.

"I care about all of it, you know."

She peeked up at him, over her macaroni. "All of what?"

"Not just the baby. You. I know you want to stay sharp in your profession, so you don't want to quit your job, but…really… Avery. If you'd let me, you'd never have to work another day in your life."

She studied him. This time the offer of money wasn't condescending or out of place. It was his reaction to touching his child, albeit through her skin. And it was equal parts of moving and silly.

"Don't let him or her wrap you around their little finger already."

"What?"

"Oh, Jake. The first time he kicked I about fainted from the wonder of it. You're drunk on happiness, awe, the joy of feeling your child for the first time."

"It's pretty awe-inspiring."

"Yes. But at the end of the day, he or she is going to poop and spit up, cry all night, get skinned knees, ask for a car before he's ready, be a moody teen and probably get into trouble somewhere along the way. Maybe even big trouble."

He laughed. "Well, that certainly sucks all the mystery out of it."

"I'm just trying to show you that this is real, not fantasy."

"I get it." He ate a bite of steak, then quietly cleared his throat. "But if you wouldn't mind, I'd like to hang on to the joy a bit."

"Are you telling me I'm too much of a realist?"

"You're too much of an arguer…too much of a lawyer. Always looking for something wrong or something to defend. Do you know that Pete spends most of his time spelling out what could go wrong with all my projects, all my deals, all my interactions?"

"That's a lawyer's job."

He leaned back and laughed. "My point exactly."

She'd never thought about it like that before, but what he'd said was true. She did look for trouble. Maybe because her teenage years had been so full of it with her dad's arrest and conviction.

"Huh."

Jake watched Avery's pretty face contort as she seemed to think that through. "What? No argument? You're actually considering it?"

"Sort of."

She spooned more macaroni into her mouth and his heart took a flip. As ridiculously antiquated as it was, he felt a powerful pride at feeding her, providing for her, and he suddenly knew that if he pushed this and demanded she recognize she always argued with him, no matter what he said, she'd shut down again.

Somehow a window or door of cooperation had opened and he did not want to see it close. In fact, if it killed him, he intended to keep it open.

The wonder of having felt his child move rolled through him again in a warm wave. He owed that to her. He'd have never thought to ask to feel the baby move. He had no experience with pregnancy. But she'd given him the opportunity. He wanted this cooperation to continue.

They finished their dinner and he tried to think of small talk, but none came. How did a couple top sharing the experience of feeling their child moving? A soft glow filled him, mellowed him. They couldn't talk about it any more than they already had. But he still wanted to savor it.

So, he rose from the table. "If you'll excuse me, I'm going to my room."

"It's only seven thirty, our time."

"I know. I'll watch a little television and hope to fall asleep because morning is going to be here really quickly."

She gave him a polite smile. "Sure. I'll watch some TV too. It'll be fun trying to figure out what they're saying since everything's probably going to be in French."

He could have suggested they watch together so he could translate for her, but he didn't want to risk his good mood—or *hers*. He *liked* getting along with her and maybe he wanted to savor that, too.

"Good night."

"Good night."

He turned to walk to his room but before he was halfway there, she said, "By the way, what should I wear to meet your mother?"

He faced her, catching the gaze of her stunning emerald eyes. He'd seen her dressed up, dressed down, naked. With hair up, hair down, hair a mess. She always stole his breath. That was what had gotten him into trouble with her. They hadn't needed to talk, hadn't needed to be friends. He just loved looking at her, touching her. And now they had no common ground, except their baby.

"You could dress up if you like. But really, just take off that robe and put on a pair of pants and you'd be fine."

She winced. "You noticed I didn't have pants on?"

"Hard not to when you showed me your

belly. I didn't question it, just figured you wanted to be comfortable." He shrugged as if it was no big deal, but if the awe at feeling his child move hadn't overwhelmed him, he would have been annihilated by her bare legs.

She rose from the table too. "Okay." She turned and headed to her room then spun around again. "Is your mom expecting us?"

"Before we left New York, I had one of my assistants let her know I'd be meeting her tomorrow morning after breakfast, and I told the front desk here to call her to let her know we'd arrived. She's in a nearby hotel. I wanted to put a little space between us to give us some breathing room."

She nodded. "Okay. Good night."

He smiled and watched as she walked away, then raced to his room. They'd had an hour of normal conversation. She'd shown him the baby, let him feel his child move. And tomorrow morning, he was going to lead her into his mother's suite, like a lamb to the slaughter?

That would ruin every good thing that had happened between them. Control freak that he was, he refused to lose the good will she was showing him, and there was only one way to soften that awkward meeting.

He pulled out his cell phone and video called his mom.

When she answered, her face appeared on his screen. "Jake? Don't tell me you're phoning to cancel tomorrow morning. I bowed out of a spa trip with my friends to see you. You said it was urgent."

"It is. Look, Mom, I'm going to tell you something and I don't want you to go bananas."

She lifted her aristocratic nose as she fluffed out her perfectly coiffed yellow hair. "I don't go bananas."

"You're going to when you hear this… I just found out I'm going to be a dad."

Her eyes widened. "What?"

"An old girlfriend is pregnant."

Her mouth fell open, then closed, then fell open again.

"You're going to be a grandmother."

"Oh, my God!"

"I came here to tell you that, with Avery, but I suddenly realized it wasn't fair to either of you to have that kind of awkward meeting. I'm telling you now so that when we come to your suite tomorrow morning, you can be nice to her."

Her head rose as her spine stiffened. "I'm always nice."

"You're always proper."

"I'm thrilled at becoming a grandmother."

"Yes. Well, you don't know the whole story. Avery is six months pregnant."

Her mouth fell open again. "And you're only telling me now!"

"I just found out myself."

"Oh." She blinked long lashes over her perfect sky-blue eyes. "You know what? It doesn't matter." She pulled in a shivery breath. "I'm going to be a grandmother."

He laughed. "Yes."

"We'll have a baby to spoil."

"Maybe not spoil. Avery's very down-to-earth."

"Is she pretty? Is our grandchild going to be beautiful because their mother is beautiful?"

"Hey, I had a hand in this too."

"I know that, dear, but take your good genes and add a beautiful mother and we could end up with a stunning child."

He laughed. "You're okay with this?"

"Okay? For Pete's sake, Mr. Worry Wart, I'm over the moon. Since your father's death I've been so out of sorts." She stopped, sucked in a breath and totally changed the subject, obviously not wanting to talk about her husband dying. "I'd planned on having only coffee for our visit tomorrow. I'll need to get something else. What does she drink? Soda? Water?"

"She seems to like apple juice."

"Then that's what I'll get. I'll see you tomorrow."

He hung up the phone surprised at how well that had gone, then he groaned. His mother might be thrilled, but there was no way in hell she'd let Avery off the hook for keeping the pregnancy from them. She'd say something—

Well, if she did he would be in the room with them and he would smooth it over.

He groaned. Really? In the plane, he'd insulted her over using her laptop. He really didn't know enough about her to know what smoothed things over or riled her even more. In fact, he was pretty good at riling her. And in spite of his attempt to fix things with his mom, seeing her tomorrow morning could still be a disaster.

For Avery, meeting Jake's mom was like getting an audience with the queen.

When Jake knocked on the door of his mother's suite at the plush Le Bristol hotel, a maid answered. She led them from the entryway into a sitting room with a view of the city. Maureen McCallan sat on a Queen Anne chair to the right of a sofa. Her yellow hair had been styled in a perfect chignon. Her black dress and pearls screamed high society. *Old-school* high society.

Avery gave a silent prayer of thanks that she'd put on the dress she'd packed. The pretty royal blue sheath brought out the best in her coloring and though it didn't exactly hide her stomach, it didn't accent it either.

Mrs. McCallan waited for Jake to walk over and lean down to kiss her perfectly powdered cheek.

"Mom. You look great."

"Even one day in Paris works wonders." She looked at Avery. "And who is this?"

"I'm Avery Novak, Mrs. McCallan," Avery said, stepping in to shake her hand.

His mom took the hand Avery offered, but she smiled coolly as she glanced at Avery's belly. "It looks like you have something to tell me."

Jake said, "Mom!"

His mom took a long, deep breath. "So... I'm going to be a grandmother?"

"Yes."

Her lips twisted as she tried to hold back a smile. "Really? Have you done a DNA test?"

Jake shook his head, clearly annoyed, but said, "Avery would sometimes rather wrestle a bear than be in the same room with me. If this wasn't my baby, we wouldn't be here right now."

Maureen laughed. "So what is it you don't like, Avery? Our money, our lifestyle, our name?"

"All of them, ma'am, except the name. Nothing wrong with the name McCallan."

"At least you have the decency to be honest."

"Oh, she'll be decent like that more than any of us really wants."

"Good. I like knowing what or whom I'm dealing with." She rose from the chair. "Now, we were supposed to have coffee, but you can't drink coffee," she said to Avery as she walked to a discreet bar in the corner where a silver tea service sat on a silver tray. "I do however have an assortment of juices. What would you like?"

"Apple if you have it."

"Apple it is."

She brought coffee and juice over to Jake and Avery who had settled on a comfortable blue sofa, then returned to her Queen Anne chair.

"Tell me everything."

Avery held back a wince. "There's not much to tell."

"Did you have morning sickness?"

"Horribly."

Maureen clapped her hands. "Oh, that's great. Legend in our family is that morning sickness means your child will have a head full of hair."

Avery fingered her own thick hair. "If he's

anything like me, he won't have to worry about that."

Maureen gasped. "He? You know it's a boy?"

"No. It's just easier to say *he* rather than *he or she* all the time."

"Too bad. I'd like a boy." Maureen stopped and smiled. "But a little girl would be so much fun. Imagine the clothes we could buy for her!"

"Mom, Avery may not want us to overindulge her."

"I'm returning to my home in Pennsylvania," Avery said. "It's a small town. She might not want to be wearing party dresses and tiaras."

Maureen laughed. "I was thinking more along the line of tights and long tops. Saw the cutest outfit the other day in the park. A baby had on caramel-colored tights with a giraffe-print top. So cute."

Avery smiled. "It sounds cute." It really did and it also didn't seem over-the-top or off-the-wall. "I've always been a sucker for black patent leather Mary Janes."

"Oh, I love those." Maureen smiled at Avery then said, "You really have to move to Pennsylvania?"

Jake said, "She's starting a law practice in her hometown."

"Oh."

"I wouldn't ever deprive you the chance of seeing your grandchild though." The words spilled out, a combination of Avery's guilt over keeping the pregnancy a secret and the realization that she'd deprived Jake's family. "Pennsylvania's not that far away."

"No. It isn't," Maureen said congenially.

Avery almost relaxed, but the memory of meeting her dad's boss at company picnics rose in her brain. Paul Barnes had been the epitome of politeness. He'd played softball, made ice cream sundaes for the kids and doled out the mashed potatoes for the evening buffet.

But he hadn't had an ounce of compassion for her father. He hadn't even considered that her dad had been telling the truth when he said he hadn't stolen the money missing from their accounts. When evidence came up that proved he was innocent, Barnes hadn't believed it. He'd contested her father getting a new trial.

She told herself to stop being suspicious and tried to push the memory of six poverty-stricken years out of her head, as she smiled at Jake's mom. She relayed the baby's due date, her doctor's name and the hospital where she planned to give birth.

"Would it be too much to ask for me to be there?"

Avery laughed. "The labor room is fine, but I don't want anybody in the delivery room."

Maureen laughed. "I'll take what I can get." She rose from her chair. "I hate to push you out but I'm having lunch with friends and need to change."

Jake rose too and turned to offer Avery a hand to stand. "That's fine. We were planning on heading home anyway."

"Heading home? We barely had a chance to talk! Besides, you have a ball on Saturday."

"I decided to skip it, so I can get Avery home."

Maureen said, "You'll do no such thing." She pulled in a breath and faced Avery. "Avery, have you ever seen Paris?"

"No."

"Fabulous. Jake can show you around today. We can have dinner tonight at eight and tomorrow we'll all go to the ball together."

Jake said, "Mom, Avery has things to attend to—"

But Avery interrupted him. She knew his mom would probably come up with a million questions today and she'd want to talk again tonight. She owed the woman that much. Plus, she really, really wanted to see Paris.

"I'd actually like to tour the city."

Jake caught her gaze. "Really?"

She laughed. "I'm starting a law firm that

helps people who fall between the cracks of public defenders and high-priced counsel. I'm not going to have money for travel. This will probably be the only time I'm in Paris. I'd like to see at least some of it."

Maureen clapped her hands together. "That's fabulous! Meet me here around seven-thirty for drinks."

CHAPTER SIX

THEY STEPPED OUT of Le Bristol, onto the quiet street. Jake sucked in a long breath. "Thank you."

She faced him, her smile lighting her eyes. He could have stared into those green orbs forever, but she said, "For what?"

He broke the spell by looking away. "For agreeing to stay."

She laughed. "I meant what I said about wanting to see Paris."

He supposed that could be true, but there was more behind what she'd done than a desire to see the city. She hadn't merely been kind to his mother; she'd been respectful. And so open about everything that his mother had been like her old self. He hadn't seen that happiness on his mother's face since before his father's death.

He'd never realized a grandchild would turn her mood around, then wondered why he hadn't. She needed something in her life right now. Someone to love. And what better than a baby?

His appreciation for Avery's kindness multiplied exponentially.

"I'll be happy to show you Paris. I'm at your disposal for the whole day."

They reached the corner of the hotel. With their view unobstructed, they could see the Eiffel Tower.

She gasped. "That's what I want to see."

He said, "Okay," and pulled out his phone to call for a car, but she stopped him.

"Why don't we walk?"

He gaped at her. "Walk?" He switched screens on his phone and began searching for the distance from the Bristol to the Eiffel Tower. "I know it looks like it's just right over there." The answer popped up and he displayed the phone to her. "But it's almost two miles."

She shrugged. "So? I want to see Paris, but I don't just want to see things like the Eiffel Tower. I want to see *Paris*. Walk the streets." She pulled in a long drink of air. "Breathe in the smells." She sniffed again. "What *is* that?"

He laughed. "Any one of a number of restaurants." The temptation to take her hand rose in him. The impulse was so natural it would have made him caution himself about appreciating Avery so much that he did something stupid, except they'd dated. Three weeks might not seem like a long time, but it had set precedents, habits that were slowly seeping into their association again.

Especially since they were getting along. All he'd remembered from their time together was sex and arguments over politics. But now that they were getting along, the arguments faded into nothing and memories of how soft she was rolled through him.

Morning sun poured down on them. The scents, sights and sounds of Paris flowed around them. Resisting the urge to hold her hand, he motioned for her to start walking.

They bumped along with other tourists, glancing around, took a side street or two, bobbed in and out of shops along the way, not really saying anything. When they came to the Gagosian Gallery, she stopped.

"This is what I'm talking about. Walking, we'll find things like this and can pop in and have a look around."

It wasn't what he'd usually do. He liked plans. He didn't just "pop into" art galleries or museums any more than he'd think he could pop into the ballet. But he was resisting their attraction and they weren't arguing, so why spoil it?

In fact, he was beginning to wonder if he shouldn't try to use it. Rather than walk silently through the streets, they could be talking. Learning about each other. She'd already told him about her dad. He knew about her job from Pete Waters. But she knew virtually nothing about him.

Which might be why she constantly drew all the wrong conclusions.

He opened the door for her and they entered. He knew the exhibits changed regularly, so he wasn't sure what they would find. Today, bright paintings stood out in stark contrast against white walls. She gazed around with a look of such wonder that he laughed.

"You like?"

She glanced at him. "You don't?"

And here was his first chance to tell her something about himself. "When it comes to art, I'm a take-it-or-leave-it kind of guy."

She ducked into the first exhibit. "You're telling me you don't like art?"

"I prefer practical things over showy. Things like sofas and cabinets. A cleverly arranged kitchen. That's art to me."

She paused in front of a painting, but looked at him. "I get that you're practical, but a kitchen as art? Really?"

"I cook."

She laughed. "You make bagels."

He shook his head. "Nope. Learned to cook when I was at university, so I wouldn't starve."

She scoffed. "Right." Her gaze took a trip down his proper navy blue blazer and gray trousers. "Like a McCallan would ever starve."

It wasn't the first time one of her digs had gotten to him. But it was the first time he realized sidestepping her insults had kept them from getting to know each other. She thought the rich had it so easy? Well, she hadn't lived with his father.

"While I was at university, my father made me live on an allowance that was just barely enough to get by for a month. I quickly discovered how much cheaper it was to cook for myself than eat out, and started making my own breakfast, lunch and dinner. I also started saving chunks of each month's deposit."

She stopped walking and genuinely seemed interested. "I get the cooking but why save some of your allowance?"

"Because my dad had a tendency to do odd things at the drop of a hat. I went to the house for dinner on Friday nights and one Friday he got it in his head that I was pampered. The next month he withheld my allowance to teach me coping skills."

She stared at him. "He held back the money you depended on to live?"

He sniffed a laugh. "More than once. And he didn't just do that to me. When my brother Seth entered university, Dad did it to him too. It sounds crazy—" It was crazy and cruel and arbitrary, and just thinking about it filled his veins with the fire of anger, but this was his life. Probably the most important thing he could tell her so she could get to know him. "But in my father's mind, he was teaching us discipline and street smarts."

"It sounds like a mind game to me."

Surprised that she hadn't sided with his dad and agreed that pampered sons needed to be taught lessons, he said, "What he did was capricious and bordered on cruel. My brother Seth didn't catch on as quickly as I did and spent a month homeless."

This time she gaped at him. "What?"

"You heard me."

"I can't believe your mom would allow that!"

"She didn't know. It was sort of a point of pride for us not to tell her." They ambled to another painting. In this one reds, yellows and oranges mixed and mingled in such a way that it reminded him of the fire of hell. Or maybe it was talking about his father, remembering the difficulties of his and Seth's childhood.

"He broke Seth."

"Broke him?"

"My dad pushed us too hard and too far. Berating us for an A that he thought should have been an A-plus. Refusing to pay tuition. And when we got jobs—realizing the only way to have any security was to earn our own money—he'd raid our bank accounts, taking money we'd earned. There was no such thing as security in our lives. I learned not to put my check in the bank, to pay cash for things like rent and to hide any extra money under my mattress. I learned to combat my father's impulses with plans and logic.

"Seth's senior year he couldn't handle it anymore. The fact that our father had friends in places that allowed him to steal from our accounts broke him. He dropped out of university, disappeared for the longest time. When he finally got in touch with me two years later, he was working for a brokerage firm during the day and going to school at night, living with two roommates, incredibly happy."

She held his gaze. Her green eyes soft with sympathy. "Oh."

He shook his head; the last thing he wanted was her pity. "I don't want you to feel sorry for me. I just thought if we knew a thing or two about each other, maybe we'd get along."

She nodded, but he still saw the sympathy in her eyes.

"Seth is very successful now. He works for McCallan, Inc., but he just sold half of a brokerage firm he started with another friend. He's very happy."

She only continued to stare at him.

He frowned. "It shocks you to hear how Seth made his own way? Or to hear that our lives weren't exactly easy?"

"No. I'm standing here wondering if Seth gave up, how much guts did it take for you to stay?"

"Guts?"

"No matter how difficult leaving seemed, staying was probably a hundred times harder."

His chest softened with something he could neither define nor describe. He'd never told his mother about the things his father had done to him and Seth. He'd never told her about the double dealings and deceit he'd found at McCallan, Inc. when he'd gone to work for the company. And really, he hadn't told Avery either, not the whole of it, not the worry or the strength it took to be one step ahead of his dad, yet she understood.

He didn't think anyone would ever understand.

"I couldn't leave. I always knew I'd be the one to take over the family business. I had no idea my father would die this soon and that I'd barely be in my thirties before I was running it all, but I had a responsibility."

She continued to hold his gaze. "Yes, you did."

"And Seth is back. Willing to do his fair share."

"But the responsibility rests on your shoulders."

"Someone has to lead. Besides, I like who I am. I like that when I went to work for my dad, I saw Seth and I weren't the only ones he bullied. He hurt lots of people with his quick temper and snap judgments."

"It's why you're so logical."

He sniffed a laugh. "Yes. But the bottom line is I forced him to clean up his act and basically restored the family name. Still, if you look in our closet, you're going to find plenty of skeletons."

"Is that why you agreed not to use my father's conviction against me?"

"No." Because they'd reached the end of the exhibits, he put his hand on her arm and ushered her toward the door. "I agreed to that because I don't believe what your dad did or didn't do has any bearing on our child."

"He's innocent."

"Exactly. And he's still our baby's grandfather. Just as I want my mother to be a part of our child's life, your parents need to be a part of it too."

He opened the door for her and they walked outside into the sunshine, stepping around a gaggle of happy tourists who looked at brochures, studied maps and laughed together.

As Jake and Avery headed up the street, he said, "Good or bad, every child needs to know his full heritage."

She stopped and took a quiet breath. "I'm not sure how that's going to happen with me living in Pennsylvania."

Her honesty hit him right in the heart. "We'll work it out." He met her gaze. For the first time in their history, they'd held a conversation that hadn't ended in an argument. "See how we're talking now? Open-mindedly and realistically. That's how we'll figure it out."

She nodded.

"But for now—" He looked around. "It is an absolutely beautiful day in Paris." His good mood restored, as thoughts of his father flitted away and spontaneously seeing the city seemed like a great idea. "We'll stroll up to the Eiffel Tower, find a nice bistro for lunch and then stroll some more."

"You do realize you just planned our entire afternoon."

Disappointment that he'd totally misread spontaneity filled him. "Really?"

"It's okay. Except…" She raised her foot enough to show him her high heels. "These are fine now, but in another hour or so I'm going to want to toss them in the Seine."

He laughed. "So we need to go back to the hotel?"

Avery said, "Yes. Thank you." But her head still spun over what he'd told her and how she didn't know him at all.

Though she now understood why he was so stuffy, so careful about everything he did, she'd never even considered how strong he was. She hated that his father had been cruel to him, but loved that he seemed to have found his way—and was happy. She was also glad that he'd trusted her enough to confide in her. Because she suspected this story wasn't something he told everyone.

Uneasiness unexpectedly tightened her chest. She liked having his trust, but it suddenly made her feel close to him. He wasn't just a stuffy guy she'd dated six months ago. He was someone she was getting to know.

But wasn't that good? After all, they had a lot to iron out about the baby.

"What do you say we change now?"

Pulled out of her thoughts, she said, "What?"

"Change now. Not wait until after lunch. Let's be comfortable. Let's enjoy this."

She smiled at him and he smiled back. For ten seconds she didn't hear the sounds of the tourists and buses. She didn't hear the birds or the traffic. She simply looked into his eyes. He was such a good-looking guy that she wasn't surprised by the sizzle of attraction that raced from her chest to her toes and back up again. But this time, she felt a connection form. A real one. Because it was smart to get to know each other, to be reasonable with each other, she decided that was good too.

"Okay."

They returned to their hotel to put on comfortable shoes and jeans and T-shirts. Avery immediately felt more like herself. And, Jake? Well, he looked totally different. But having heard his story it seemed appropriate that he look different. Carefree, even though she knew he wasn't. But maybe for today he could be?

"Now, weren't we planning to walk to the Eiffel Tower?"

"Yes. I'd love to see the Eiffel Tower." She'd also love to see him relax. Completely. And enjoy the day.

"Let's go then."

They rode down in the elevator and walked outside, this time looking like two ordinary tourists. He reached for her hand, then tucked it into the crook of his elbow. The gesture was so casual, yet so intimate, that it threw her.

As easily as possible, she pulled her hand away. "You don't have to hold on to me. I'm fine."

"I don't want to lose you. Not that I think you'll get lost." He winced. "Honestly, I just don't want you to fall."

She shook her head, but had to admit it was cute that he was so concerned about her. Except it gave her an odd feeling. The sense that the real Jake was hovering just under the surface of the man she knew. And with the right word or situation, his facade would crack and she'd be face to face with—what? A nice guy?

That could be stretching things. He might have had a totally different childhood than she'd believed, but that childhood had made him who he was. Too cautious. Too careful. Very guarded.

Getting to know him didn't mean she'd like him.

She brushed her hair out of her eyes. "I'm pregnant not sick."

He held up his hands in surrender. "Okay, I get it." He glanced down at her tennis shoes. "And you look ready to walk. Let's go."

They meandered to the Eiffel Tower, enjoying the sunny afternoon. The sight of the city from the tower took her breath away. After a little more walking, followed by a boat ride on the Seine, they had a late lunch in a bistro. Through their meal, they listened to the sounds of the city, breathed in the scents swirling in the air and filled themselves with sandwiches with crusty bread and salads that made her groan in ecstasy.

But after that she was tired. They returned to the hotel and she immediately fell asleep. When she woke, she realized the only thing she had to wear to dinner was the dress she'd worn that morning.

All the fun they'd had together melted away into reality. They might have spent a great day, but there was no worry that something would happen between them—no matter how sweet he was when his guard was down. When it came to things like dressing for dinner, they were on two different pages.

For a second she felt awkward having to wear the same clothes, but she lifted her chin.

There was nothing wrong with the sheath. It was pretty, and sufficiently fancy. Sure, she'd worn it that morning, but it didn't smell. If Jake or his mother didn't like her wearing the same dress, they would simply have to get over it.

Still, she pulled her hair to the top of her head, fixing it in a loose knot with tendrils trailing down her neck and near her ears to at least make the dress look a little more elegant. Then she slipped into the only jacket she'd brought, the black blazer she'd worn on the flight over.

When she stepped out of her bedroom, Jake was already in the sitting room wearing a black suit and red tie, about the same level of formal as her dress, but not the same clothes he'd had on that morning.

"You look wonderful."

Heat rose to her cheeks. "Thanks."

"I like your hair like that."

She sucked in a breath. Even if he was only saying that to be nice, she appreciated it. "Yeah, me too."

He directed her to the door and opened it for her. When they stepped out of the lobby, onto the street, he waggled his eyebrows at her. "Want to walk?"

"To the Bristol?" She laughed and displayed her high heels again. "Shoes."

"Got it."

He nodded at a driver standing in front of a black limo and the man jumped to attention, opening the back door for them. The limo was obviously Jake's, in spite of his suggestion that they walk—

Which meant he'd *teased* her?

She shouldn't have been pleased, but she was. Not because it broke the ice, but because he'd made a joke.

A joke.

From the stuffiest man she'd ever met.

A man who had been emotionally abused by his dad.

A man who worried about her.

As the connections piled up, she ignored the nagging sense of menace that accompanied them. They *needed* to get along to raise a baby together. Hell, they needed to get along to figure out visitation. Getting comfortable with each other was good.

They arrived at his mother's suite and while Maureen sipped a cocktail and Jake drank a beer, Avery sat on the sofa talking about the pregnancy, the baby, her plans.

Maureen listened, nodding, laughing in all the right places and not once mentioning Avery's dress.

They went to the restaurant his mom had

chosen only to find she'd invited two of her girlfriends to join them. They hugged Avery and clucked over her, and through the first two courses made her feel like the only woman to ever have a baby.

Over beef Wellington, they started talking about their own pregnancies. Somehow that shifted into a discussion of maternity clothes and how styles had changed and how a woman now at least had a shot at getting a decent gown for a ball.

"You are coming to tomorrow night's charity event, aren't you?"

Annalise Jones asked the question innocently, and Jake casually said, "No. We're going back to New York tomorrow."

But his mother gasped. "Back? Tomorrow? Jake, you promised me you would attend this year!"

"And Avery needs to get home."

Avery looked at Jake. "You're not going because of me?"

"I don't want to impose any more than we have."

"But you'd like to go?"

He shrugged. "The hospitals and homes being funded do good work." He shrugged again. "It might be interesting to meet the people who run them."

"You should go."

"I'm not leaving you alone at the hotel while I attend a ball."

She'd thought he'd offer her the use of the family jet to return to New York the next day, but before she could say anything, Julianna, Maureen's short round friend, spoke up.

"Bring her to the ball. You buy two tickets every year. You should use them."

Avery said, "I don't have anything to wear," at the same time Jake said, "She'll be tired."

"Oh, nonsense," Maureen said. She faced Avery, "We can get you a dress." Then she looked at Jake. "And you can take her home early. It's not like you have to stay at the ball all night. I just have some people I want you to meet."

CHAPTER SEVEN

IN THE END, they agreed to go. In the limo ride back to their hotel, Jake politely turned to Avery.

"You can bow out if you want. You can even take the McCallan jet home tomorrow." He didn't want her to go. He wanted her to stay. Maybe a little more than he should. "I know you're eager to get back to your job."

She shook her head. "I don't think I have a job anymore."

"If I gave you that impression, I'm sorry. Pete never said you were fired, just that you couldn't work on McCallan cases."

She shook her head again. "Conflict of interest stretches beyond me staying away from your cases. When I go to work on Monday morning, I'm going to get a speech on—" She lowered her voice to sound like Pete. "Even the appearance of impropriety." She brought her voice back to normal. "And he'll be right."

"So, you're unemployed?"

"Probably. And I might as well go to the ball." She glanced over at him. "Just how fancy does this thing get?"

"I've never been. You'll have to talk to my mom." He winced. "She'll probably be happy to take you shopping."

"Another hit to my savings."

"No. This one is on me. You wouldn't be going if we weren't in Paris. And you wouldn't be in Paris if I hadn't brought you here."

"I can pay for it."

"So can I."

The limo stopped in front of their hotel. Jake exited and helped Avery slide out. The night air was cool as they walked to the hotel door.

Hands in his trouser pockets, beside her but with two feet separating them, he felt the strangest sensation. Not quite that he needed to help her walk. More like he wanted to be close to her. She was the mother of his child. She'd been incredibly sweet to his mother. And when she smiled at him, his stomach plummeted, his breath shimmied in his chest.

He'd never felt this kind of connection before. But it was like a mirage. One second it was there and the next it wasn't. It never hung around long enough for him to figure out what it was.

Telling himself he was all kinds of crazy, he walked her through the quiet lobby. They rode up in the elevator in silence and parted ways in the sitting room.

But he barely slept. Not only had he told her his biggest secret in the name of getting to know each other, but the way she'd treated his mom proved she was a good person, a kind person. Somehow, he'd missed that when they'd been dating. But now that he was seeing it, everything he thought he knew about her shifted, changed—nagged at him.

He didn't fall asleep until almost five. By the time he woke up around eleven, she was gone. A note on the breakfast cart left by room service told him that his mother had sent a car to pick her up to go shopping.

He yanked his phone off his bedside table and hit the contact key for his mother. When she answered, he said, "Do not let her pay for her gown."

His mother laughed. "Are you kidding? I would buy the mother of my grandchild the sun, the moon and all the stars if she'd let me. She's in good hands."

"I take it she's not with you."

"She's in the fitting room, trying on the lovely white dress. Reminds me of a wedding dress."

"Mom!"

The hair on the back of his neck stood on end. And he knew why he'd been feeling so odd that he couldn't sleep. When he first discovered Avery was pregnant, there was no chance in hell anything would happen between them. Now, everything felt different. The sexy woman of his dreams was merging with real Avery...and he liked her.

And it meant something.

Or it didn't. They needed to figure that out.

"I'm just describing the gown, dear. Oh, there she is now. I'll talk to you later."

Avery stepped out of the fitting room and onto the platform in front of the three mirrors designed to show her how the dress flowed from every angle.

She frowned, then glanced back at Jake's mom. "It looks like a wedding dress."

Maureen smiled. "It does. Isn't it lovely? And aren't you lovely?"

Avery laughed. She wouldn't call out Maureen, but she saw what was going on. "I'm attending a ball, not my wedding." She turned to the sales clerk. "Do you have something in a creamy, peach or coral color?"

"Of course."

The sales girl scampered away, and Maureen clapped her hands together. "I'll bet peach looks absolutely gorgeous on you with your red hair."

Avery stepped down off the platform. "If we get the right shade, it's my best color."

Maureen rose. "Do you need help getting out of that?"

"No. I'm fine." She turned to go into the dressing room, but paused and looked at herself in the mirror one more time. "It is pretty, though, isn't it?"

"You're going to make somebody a beautiful bride."

"Maybe." She took in the elegant white gown one more time. "But probably not."

"Oh, sweetie! Don't say that!"

"I'm committed to my work, Maureen. And the baby." She laid her hand on her stomach. "Not sure there's going to be enough time left for a man or a marriage."

Maureen picked up the back of the white gown and followed Avery into the fitting room. "I've found that in life people make time for the things that are important."

"You sound like my mom."

"That's because older ladies are very smart. We have a handbook."

Avery burst out laughing.

Maureen tugged down the zipper of the dress, then slipped out of the small room.

After the door closed behind her, Avery took off the gown. She was wrestling it back onto the hanger when the sales clerk returned with two wonderful peach-colored dresses.

She looked at the first and said, "Let's try this one." The off-the-shoulder style and criss-cross beading on the bodice would draw everyone's eye to her top, not her belly. Plus, the skirt of the gown was loose enough that it wouldn't hug her baby bump, but not so loose that it belled out. The chiffon fabric simply flowed from her waist to the floor.

The sales clerk helped her into the dress. When Avery saw herself in the mirror, she knew there was no need to try on the second one. Maureen agreed. A few minor alterations were required to the top, and the sales clerk arranged to have the gown nipped and tucked and shipped to Avery's hotel that afternoon.

When they stepped out into the sunshine, Maureen breathed deeply. "That was fun. We should do it again. Maybe shop for baby clothes together."

Avery said, "Sure." Mostly because she'd be unemployed in New York until the baby was born. It was an easy way for Maureen to be involved and a great way for Avery to supervise what she bought.

They headed to the waiting limo, but Maureen stopped abruptly. "You said you don't know the baby's sex, but I think we should find out. It'll make everything easier. Especially for people who want to buy gifts." She gasped. "And the nursery."

The driver opened the limo door. As she climbed in, Avery said, "I don't want to know the baby's sex until it's born. I want the surprise. I'd planned on making the nursery navy blue and gray, then adding a splash of pink or light blue depending on the sex of the baby."

Maureen nodded. "I like it."

"You're not upset about not knowing the sex of the baby before it's born?"

She considered that. "It would make things easier, but I'm trying to decide if I like being able to buy the right clothes or if the excitement of finding out the baby's sex at the hospital will be more fun."

The driver got into the limo and pulled out into the street.

Avery said, "I like the old-fashioned way."

"Really? You seem like such a modern girl."

"I am. Sometimes I even get a little too far out with my thinking. But my parents are very down-to-earth. They keep me grounded."

"Interesting. Jake's down-to-earth too. I remember something my dad used to say about opposites being good for each other. Something about balance. Anyway, Tom and I were opposites. He kept me from flying off to the moon and I kept him from being too hard on the kids."

Avery had to fight to stop a gasp. Her husband had been extremely hard on his sons. He'd hidden that from Maureen, but it wasn't Avery's place to tell her. She hadn't made a commitment to Jake not to tell his mom—or anyone—any of the things he'd told her about his father. He hadn't asked her to keep a secret, but in her heart, she suddenly realized that he'd trusted that she would.

He'd trusted her with probably the biggest secret of his life.

Maureen walked her into the lobby of her hotel and after a quick kiss on the cheek, Avery rode up the elevator and ambled back the hall to their suite.

When she opened the door, Jake spun away from the window to face her. His cheeks bore the black stubble of a day's growth of beard. His hair was a mess. If his room hadn't been dead silent that morning as she'd eaten breakfast, she'd think he hadn't slept.

Their gazes caught. The warmth of familiarity washed through her. She'd learned more about this guy, the father of her child, in the past twenty-four hours than she had in three weeks of dating—three weeks of sex without intimacy.

Awkwardness filled the room. He'd shown her Paris. Made her laugh. Told her a secret that she'd vowed not to share without once ever saying a word. Now he looked like he'd been through a war.

"I found my dress."

"Good."

She pointed at her bedroom, a room of safety where she could think some of this through. "If you don't mind, I'm getting used to having a nap every day."

He laughed. "Go ahead. I've got some work I need to do." He paused. "If I can use your laptop again?"

Grateful that he'd be busy, she said, "Sure," ran into her bedroom, retrieved the laptop and handed it to him.

"Not going to set it to my screen name?"

"No." She caught his gaze. "I trust you."

That was the whole hell of it. She did.

He trusted her. She trusted him.

What had Paris done to them?

CHAPTER EIGHT

AVERY DIDN'T COME out of her bedroom all afternoon. Around six o'clock, Jake walked over to knock on her door to make sure she was okay, but a bad feeling swirled through him when he raised his hand to the white wood. He was concerned about her, but she was clearly avoiding him.

Did he really want to interrupt her when she didn't want to see him? Since they'd arrived in Paris, he'd been sensing a connection forming, but what if she hadn't?

What if he'd told her his biggest secret, relaxed with her, made jokes with her, when she'd been cringing inside, wishing she was home?

Chastising himself for making a big deal out of her avoiding him when not talking was their normal routine, he returned to his room, showered and dressed in the tux he'd brought for the ball. They weren't friends or lovers or *anything* anymore. He'd thought getting to know each other would make things easier. It appeared she didn't. It wouldn't be the first time he'd misinterpreted her. So, he would let her alone.

He exited his quarters to find her standing in the sitting room, staring out the large window with a fabulous view of the city.

Turning to face him, she quietly said, "I'm sorry I needed a little time this afternoon. I don't want you to think I didn't appreciate your generosity. I have never enjoyed two days as much as I have these past two. Thank you for giving me a chance to see the city."

He tried to say, *You're welcome*, but nothing came out. She'd shocked him. He might have opened up to her, but the only time she'd told him anything personal was when she'd negotiated about her dad. But more than that, she looked amazing, so striking, his tongue stuck to the roof of his mouth.

When he found his voice, he said, "You're welcome." He waited a beat, then couldn't hold it in any longer. "You are so beautiful."

She glanced away and began fussing with the wrap she'd brought out, unfolding it so she could slide it over her shoulders. "Thank you." She met his gaze. "Your mother paid for this, but I intend to send her a check."

He could have argued. He could have

laughed at her thinking his mother would actually cash a check when she'd meant the gown as a gift. Instead, he realized Avery was diverting his attention away from the compliment.

Something primal and male rose up in him. If he wanted to tell her she was beautiful, if he wanted to dwell on that all evening, there was nothing she could do to stop him.

"You *are* beautiful, you know."

She shook her head. "You've told me that a million times."

"In bed," he agreed. "This is different."

"So, before this, you didn't think I was beautiful with clothes on?"

He laughed. "Deflect all you want." She'd never been uncomfortable with him telling her she was beautiful. Their association back then had been light, careless. Today's compliment was personal. And whether she wanted to admit it or not, it pleased her.

"You're not going to stop my good mood tonight. I'm about to attend a party with probably the most attractive woman in the city. I intend to have fun." He motioned to the door. "Limo's waiting."

They walked down the hall without saying a word. Rode the elevator in silence. Traversed the lobby like two strangers, but when they got outside, into the music of the city, he took her hand.

As the driver opened the limo door, she wiggled her hand away before sliding onto the seat. He slid in beside her.

"So, you don't have any idea what to expect tonight."

He said no, and for once that didn't set his nerve endings on fire. He wasn't worried about his mom, thinking about the people he would meet—

He felt like dancing. The day had been a constant series of ups and downs, but having told her about his dad and having her tell him she'd enjoyed the day, he felt lighter. It was confusing and weird, but he liked it. He liked this strange feeling that for once in his life he could completely relax.

"We're just going to wing it?"

"Yes." He paused to glance at her. "I thought you would like that?"

"It'll be fine."

They didn't say anything else on the way to the hotel. He guided her toward the ballroom with one hand on her elbow and she didn't yank herself away. He considered that a win.

His mother met them two steps before they entered and walked with them through the receiving line, introducing him to heads of charities that benefited from his donation and he accepted their thanks.

Attempting to find their table, he was stopped by friends of his parents and more people on the boards of the charities who wanted to meet him.

By the time they got dinner, he was starving. He ate with gusto, then eyed the food on Avery's plate.

"Going to eat those potatoes?"

She turned to gape at him. "Who are you and what have you done with Jake McCallan?"

He laughed. "I'm just in a weird mood."

"Well, it's freaking me out."

"Why? We're in a city that's thousands of miles away from our home. You think you lost your job. I'm still reeling from discovering I'm about to be a dad." He almost told her that he'd been getting warm, fuzzy feelings about her all day, and decided that would make things weirder. "Why don't we just let go tonight?"

"You mean for once? Because I can't imagine you've ever let go before this."

"How do you know?"

"You're really bad at it."

"How can a person be bad at letting go?"

"You have tells. For most people spontaneity happens…" She paused and finally said,

"Well, spontaneously. I can see you thinking things through."

He almost pondered that but suddenly saw that was her point. "I'll get this."

She rolled her eyes. "I doubt it."

"You're also not eating your potatoes." He took her plate and exchanged it for his. "If I'm dancing, I'll need the carbs."

She laughed.

Damn it! He'd made her laugh again.

He finished her potatoes with lightning speed, then had two glasses of champagne while the directors of the boards of the charities made speeches thanking employees, volunteers and most of all, donors.

There was a ten-minute pause that felt like an intermission while waiters discreetly cleared tables and guests mingled. Then the band started to play.

He held out his hand. "Shall we?"

She almost told him no, but he looked so eager, she couldn't resist. "Sure. Why not?"

The song was a waltz. Calm. Normal. No worries about his exuberance causing a scene. In fact, he was a flawless dancer. But with his hand on her waist and her hand on his shoulder, familiar longings trickled through her. His scent brought back memories of being together. She yearned to inhale deeply, stand on her tiptoes and kiss him until he ran his hands up and down her spine——

She shook her head to clear it of that thought. Knowing she had to put her mind elsewhere, she said, "I see somebody took dance lessons."

"Yes."

He twirled them around the floor and the romance of the move almost had her swooning. He was tall, dark, handsome and she'd touched him, tasted him——

Oh, Lord. She had to get her mind off that.

"Sorry about thinking you were crazy back at the table."

"That's all right. I understand."

"You understand why I'd think you were a bit nutty or you understand why I'd feel that way?"

"There's a difference?"

"There's always a difference."

"And the lawyer is back."

The music stopped. Eager to get away from him, to stop touching him, remembering things best left alone, she stepped away. "There's nothing wrong with being precise."

"And you call me stuffy."

"Usually you are stuffy."

"But tonight, *you're* stuffy."

She wasn't about to tell him she was fighting an attraction that was driving her crazy. She'd blame pregnancy hormones except this feeling was more about remembering. And maybe making a connection. The nice guy, the *fun* guy she'd spent the day with had also been her wonderful lover.

Obviously in deference to the older crowd, the band began to play the music for a jitterbug, something she only knew because of her grandparents.

Jake caught her hands and swung them to the left, then the right, and spun her around so fast she blinked.

"What are you doing!"

"We're dancing, remember?"

"Again?" She suddenly got it. Their bodies were brushing, causing memories of making love with stuffy Jake to mingle with the reality of dancing with fun Jake. And drive her to distraction. Which meant the easy answer was to stop touching. Stop dancing. "This is a grandpa song."

"I had lessons, remember?"

"And I only know as much about this dance as I can recall from dancing with my grandfather when I was five!"

"Piece of cake for you. I'm the one who leads. You just follow."

Despite her protests, they danced a jitterbug

lively enough to get a round of applause and a few kudos from their fellow dancers.

When they returned to their table, Maureen bounced out of her chair and helped Avery to sit.

"What is wrong with you? You're the one who said she'd be tired, and instead of taking her home you dance her to death!"

Jake laughed. "I know. I'm sorry. I'm just…" He paused. "…in a weird mood."

Maureen produced a glass of apple juice. "Well, no more dancing."

Avery glanced at Jake. She was glad to be away from the memories touching him evoked, but he looked happy. Totally relaxed. For the first time ever.

She suddenly felt guilty for letting her hormones get the better of her. The guy had had a miserable childhood. She'd had a blissful one, even if her teen years had gone bad. But in spite of that, she'd always had the love of family. His father had tortured him. Surely, she could stop her reactions and let him enjoy the evening.

"It's okay. I could probably dance to another song or two."

Annalise grinned. "Or I could dance with you, Jake."

The woman had to be thirty years older than

Jake if she was a day. Though Avery wasn't jealous, per se, she didn't want him dancing with Annalise. If he was going to be happy, relaxed, it was going to be because of her—

Her heart stuttered.

Hormones and chemistry were one thing. This feeling was quite another.

She took a sip of her apple juice, fanned herself.

Jake snapped to attention. "Are you okay?"

"Yeah. Yeah. I'm fine." She wasn't. The feeling of familiarity that had scared her so much that afternoon had joined with their sexual chemistry and morphed into joy at being with him.

But only because he was behaving differently. Silly. Funny. Maybe he was happy to be with her too?

Oh, Lord. She couldn't think that way. She couldn't like him. Well, she already did like him. But she couldn't *like* him.

That would only cause complications over custody and visits after the baby was born.

So no. No liking him. No romance.

Jake knew the second Avery changed. The air around them grew strained again.

Well, that wouldn't do. Not when he was having fun. *They* were having fun.

He rose from his seat. "You know what? Maybe it is time to head back to the hotel." He wasn't a hundred percent sure what he was doing, but he did know Avery was probably tired. If he wanted to extend this night, it wouldn't be on the dance floor—or with his mother and her friends watching.

She looked up at him, her green eyes confused. "I'm fine."

"Yeah, well, we'll probably want an early start in the morning. The time difference works in our favor, but we still need to get some sleep." He pulled out her chair for her. "Annalise and Julianna, always lovely to see you." He helped Avery stand. "Mom, I'll be in touch when you get back to New York."

He didn't give his mother a chance to argue, just ushered Avery out to the coat room. As she slid into her wrap, he texted his driver and they stepped out into the unusually warm night.

"Typically, it's colder than this in Paris in September."

She smiled slightly. "Global warming."

He shoved his hands into his trouser pockets. "Probably."

The limo pulled up. Avery got inside and he followed her. They made the trip in silence but when they were a few blocks away from the hotel, he leaned forward and said, "Can you let us out here?"

The driver slowed the limo, then pulled up to the curb. As he walked around to open the door, Avery faced Jake. "What are we doing?"

"You've never walked in Paris at night."

Her brow wrinkled in confusion. "No. I guess I haven't." Her eyes clouded as she considered that, but there'd be no need to think about it, if she wasn't tempted.

He coaxed her. "It's a beautiful night. Our last night here."

The driver opened the door.

She sighed. "Okay."

They got out, and the limo pulled away. The street still bustled with tourists. It wasn't crowded, just busy enough to give the sense that they were part of something bigger than themselves.

He slid her hand beneath his arm and tucked it into the crook of his elbow. He expected her to argue, but she was too busy looking around.

"It's so beautiful here."

"And, as I mentioned, the night's warmer than usual. Seemed a shame to waste it."

"Yes." Her soft voice tiptoed into the night, as the moon tossed silvery light across the Seine like glitter. Subtle noise from the other tourists surrounded them.

He tried to think of something to say, but nothing came to him. Right now, in this minute, making her happy, making sure she didn't regret this trip, was the only thing he wanted—even if she was back to being the woman who argued with nearly everything he said.

They stayed silent, as she glanced around. "You know, when I was a little girl, before all the craziness of my dad being arrested and going to prison, I used to dream about becoming a high-powered business person in New York City and coming to Paris anytime I wanted. Maybe having my own apartment here." She laughed. "A second home."

He almost stopped walking. Was that a secret? From her? The woman who neither wanted nor needed anybody's help?

"Then I'm glad I twisted your arm to come with me."

"You didn't have to twist my arm. We made a deal, remember?"

He remembered. She'd already told him her biggest secret, but as part of a negotiation. Admitting childhood dreams was different. It was like telling him that before her father's troubles she'd wanted all the things everybody wants. What had happened to her dad had shaped her world, her goals, her dreams.

Part of him rebelled against that, if only because it wasn't fair that an event in someone else's life would form her dreams as it stole a bit of her childhood and most of her innocence.

"Even without you coming here with me, I wouldn't have used what happened to your dad against you. It's the past."

"I know that now."

Ridiculous pride filled him. His honesty had made her feel better, but she'd made him feel honest, trustworthy, good just as he was—a feeling he'd never had before.

The hotel came into view. They walked the rest of the way without speaking. He didn't want to break the mood, or think too hard about what all this might mean. He just wanted to enjoy Paris. When they stepped into the bright lights of the lobby, he was almost sorry.

Riding in the elevator, he remembered how the evening had begun, with him teasing her. Walking down the corridor to their suite, thoughts of dancing with her almost made him laugh out loud. Then she'd confided in him. For real this time. Not as part of a deal.

It had been one of the happiest nights of his life.

He opened the door and she stepped inside, immediately turning to the right to go to her room.

He didn't even think about it. He caught

her hand and twirled her around to face him, then pulled her into his arms. His lips met hers softly at first, then when she didn't protest, he deepened the kiss, opening her mouth, tasting her. His hands ran down her bare back, then smoothed up again, enjoying the feel of her luxurious skin.

She slid her arms around his neck. The kiss went on and on, as if they'd done this a million times, and in a way they had. But never like this. Never a kiss of happiness. Or joy. Or a whole jumble of confusing emotions that culminated in one thought.

What if this was love?

Real love? Not the feeling a person had when they were dating somebody with whom they were compatible. But real, honest-to-God love.

The idea was so foreign he almost stopped kissing her, but her warm lips lured him back. Tempted him to go further, faster, indulge his cravings—

And that's when the real debate began.

Did he want to fall in love with somebody he usually argued with? Someone who wanted a life totally different than the one he had planned? He'd already lost control with her. No, he'd *given up* control to please her. And that was dangerous. Not that he thought she'd use him, but they were about to negotiate the most important thing in his life: the fate of his child.

If dealing with his father had taught him anything, it was that opponents were opponents. It didn't matter if it was his father or a total stranger. One never gave up control. Never trusted someone so much that he put important things in jeopardy—

No matter how well his opponent kissed.

He pulled back, watched her eyes open, held her gaze long enough to hope that something in her pretty green orbs would ease his fears, but all he saw were her fears.

He released her. "Thank you for a lovely evening."

Her gaze clung to his. "Thank you too."

He turned and walked into his room, deciding the kiss had been the perfect way to end anything between them except parenting their child.

CHAPTER NINE

THEY RETURNED ON SUNDAY to seventy-degree temperatures in New York City. Jake had missed four days of work and was eager to get to his apartment, his computer and the forty-two messages in his phone. Avery was told via email to report directly to Pete Waters's office the next morning.

Vacation was over. And, from Jake's cool behavior on the plane, so was anything that might have been budding between them in Paris. It could have confused her, could have hurt her, except she knew Jake McCallan. The fun Jake she'd danced with was an aberration—thank goodness. She did not want to fall in love with the guy who'd probably be taking her to court.

When she arrived at Waters, Waters and Montgomery on Monday morning, Pete explained exactly what she'd expected, including reminding her of the firm's stance on "even the appearance of impropriety."

She resigned, so he didn't have to let her go, and, grateful that she had, Pete volunteered to write a glowing letter of recommendation and provide three months' severance pay—her salary right up to her due date.

Given that that was all she'd anticipated earning, it wasn't a financial hardship to leave. She returned to her condo, changed out of her work clothes and slid into sweatpants and a big T-shirt.

With a pint of ice cream in one hand and the television remote in the other, she sat on her sofa, preparing to channel surf.

She'd never had this much time off in her life. Part of her wished she'd stayed in Paris— but being that far away from home or her doctor wasn't a good idea. Just like that kiss hadn't been a good idea.

But, oh. It definitely had been a Paris kiss. Filled with passion and emotion but with an underlying—something. Maybe regret. With the way he'd pulled away and then barely spoken to her on the plane home, it was clear even he knew they couldn't get involved. Not when they hadn't resolved all their issues about the baby.

She took a bite of the chocolate, vanilla and strawberry ice cream, as the unvarnished truth poured down on her. She was pregnant, had no job and had kissed a man who would be on the opposite end of her custody battle.

But, oh, that kiss. So surprisingly romantic from such a by-the-book guy—

Was she crazy? Did she really want to be pining over someone so different than she was? Someone who had to be told how to be spontaneous? Someone who would never move to her small town—which meant she'd have to stay in New York City and give up her dream? Which would mean losing herself. Losing the person she'd worked to become since high school. Or, the more likely scenario, getting her heart broken when she left him.

Because she would leave him. She could not give up her dreams.

She spooned another bite of the ice cream, this time just chocolate and strawberry together. As the smooth flavor rolled across her taste buds, she closed her eyes in ecstasy. But that kiss wouldn't leave her brain. It had been so romantic. A kiss like they'd never shared before, if only because it had been filled with emotion.

Real emotion.

From the stuffiest guy on the planet.

She stopped that thought. Squelched it before it could take root.

That kiss played fast and loose with her heart when she needed to be stable. Getting involved with Jake was just plain foolish. Stupid. And she was neither foolish nor stupid.

The adrenaline of drawing that conclusion filled her with energy. Instead of kicking back, she should be doing something. And Lord knew, she had enough to do. She might not be working, but she had to take the Pennsylvania bar exam. She had to sell her condo. She had to move to Pennsylvania.

Well, actually, she couldn't move to Pennsylvania until after the baby was born. She wasn't switching doctors this late in the game. Still, it would take time to sell her condo and probably time for the purchaser to get a mortgage.

So maybe it was good she didn't have a job? She could call a Realtor, get the condo on the market and spend her time making sure it was spotless for showings—as she studied for the bar. It would be good to do that exclusively for three months. No job taking up her study time. No making notes, reading law, into the wee hours of the morning.

She took one last bite of vanilla mixed with chocolate, and strode to the kitchen. After returning the ice cream to the freezer, she picked up the phone and dialed the number for her

Realtor. The sooner she put her condo on the market the better.

Her agent eagerly agreed to meet her that night to get the required information and take pictures to get the condo up for sale.

Short, blonde Eileen Naugle arrived around eight, all smiles and happiness. "This place is gorgeous!" She spun away from the kitchen and grinned broadly at Avery. "I can't imagine why you'd want to sell it."

As Eileen snapped a few pictures, Avery said, "Moving back to Pennsylvania."

The agent grimaced and said, "Pennsylvania?" as if Avery was nuts.

She shrugged and pointed at her belly. "I want to raise the baby with my family."

Eileen clasped Avery's hand. "Yes. That's a good idea. You are so lucky." She glanced around the condo. "And so am I. This place is fantastic. Nicely designed." She winked at Avery. "It'll sell in a heartbeat. Did you just redo it?"

"The remodel was finished last year. But I work a lot." She walked Eileen back through the hall and motioned for her to look into the half bath. "I don't think this bathroom or the full bath for the guestroom have ever been used."

Eileen peered in and gasped. "Oh, it's lovely." She took two pictures.

Leading her to the master, Avery said, "This room is the one room of the house that got the most use. I ate out. I worked late. The only thing I really did was sleep here." *And fool around with Jake.* But there was no reason for Eileen to know that. No reason for it to pop into her head either. Anything between her and Jake was over...

Still, they were fun memories.

They arrived at the decent-sized master with the same wide-plank hardwood floors that were throughout the home. A queen bed with tufted gray headboard sat on top of a white shag area rug.

She snapped three pictures. "This is perfect."

"And, of course, the bathroom." She and Jake had had some fun times in that shower too. But instead of seeing the scene as it had happened, she pictured it with the emotional, happy Jake who'd kissed her in Paris and her chest tightened.

She had to stop thinking about it...

About him.

But dancing with him and then sharing that kiss had stirred up memories. Or maybe longings.

Which was wrong. Totally, totally wrong.

Walking inside the master bath, Eileen glanced around nodding. "This is good. You might have used it but you're a very neat person."

After Eileen took a few pictures, Avery led her back to the living room. As the Realtor removed the agency agreement from her briefcase, Avery made her a cup of coffee in her single-serve coffee maker.

She read the agreement while Eileen sipped her coffee.

"The price is based mostly on square footage and location," Eileen said. "The condition of the unit is a bonus. We can advertise as move-in ready. Though I'm not going to put it on the market yet. I have a few private clients who will want to see it first."

"That's fine," Avery said, signing the agreement. "Since I'm no longer working, just give me a call before you show it and I'll disappear for a few hours."

She rose and Eileen rose too. "This will be so much fun!"

Avery glanced around her perfect condo. The first slice of sadness hit her. Suddenly, she wasn't sure she would call it fun to be moving out, leaving the job she'd loved and the city that had somehow gotten in her blood—or the guy who was the father of her child.

As they walked to the door, she said, "Thank you for your help."

Eileen smiled. "My pleasure."

Avery opened the door and there stood Jake, hand raised as if he was about to knock. The bedroom and shower memories tumbled back, heating her face and scrambling her pulse.

Eileen smiled. "Well, hello."

Lowering his arm, Jake said, "Hello."

Avery said, "Eileen was just leaving."

But Eileen's smile grew. "You're Jake Mc-Callan, aren't you?"

Jake held out his hand to shake hers. "Yes."

"I'm Eileen Naugle." She reached into her pocket and presented her card to him. "If you ever need assistance buying or selling, I'd be happy to help you."

Jake looked at Avery. "She's a real estate agent?" His eyes narrowed. "You're putting your condo on the market?"

"I told you I was." Avery quickly turned to Eileen. Stuffy Jake was back with a vengeance. "Thank you very much. Call me if you need anything."

Eileen said, "Sure."

Avery caught Jake's arm and yanked him

into the entryway as Eileen walked to the elevator.

Closing the door, Avery sighed. "She probably feels like she just won the lottery."

"The lottery?"

"Connections are everything to real estate agents. Expect a fruit basket and a nice-to-meet-you card in your office tomorrow morning."

He didn't laugh. He didn't even smile. "I'd gotten the impression you weren't moving until after the baby was born."

"I'm not. It'll probably take a few weeks to sell the condo and then even more time for the buyer to get a mortgage."

She wanted to invite him to sit, ask him if he wanted some coffee, maybe tell him about her day, but she stifled that urge. Stuffy Jake wasn't the kind to want to hear about her day. The man who'd kissed her so eloquently in Paris hadn't flown home to New York. No matter how much she'd thought about him that afternoon, no matter how easily she superimposed fun Jake into her memories, she and the real Jake McCallan weren't a good match.

"So you'll be around?"

"If by *around* you mean will I still be living in New York, then the answer is yes."

"Good because my mother's talking about going shopping with you. She got in this afternoon." He pulled his phone from his jacket pocket. "I'm texting her number to you. She feels it would be imposing for her to be the first one to call."

Avery laughed. "That's very sweet."

"She also wants to be part of the pregnancy but she's concerned about being a nuisance."

"I'm out of a job. I resigned this morning to save Pete the trouble of letting me go. I'm getting a decent severance package, but I'm left with three months of nothing but studying for the Pennsylvania bar exam. She won't be a nuisance. She'll be a welcome break."

He frowned. "You'd welcome the chance to spend time with my mother?"

She casually said, "All my friends will be working from nine in the morning till nine at night," but she suddenly missed the man who'd danced with her at the ball. The man who'd taken her for a moonlight stroll along the Seine and kissed her in the dark, quiet sitting room between their two bedrooms.

"You'll need company?"

She nodded, wishing the company she'd be getting could be that guy from Paris.

"Great. I'll text your number to her and tell her she can call anytime."

"Yes. Breakfast, lunch, dinner, shopping. I'll need breaks between long bouts of studying. Tell her I'm open to just about anything." She paused. "Except having her pay for everything. Sometimes she's got to let me pick up a check."

"She can do that."

"Okay then."

"Okay."

She walked him to the door, opened it for him. "Good night."

"Good night."

The air between them stilled. She remembered how he'd caught her hand, twirled her around, pulled her into his arms and kissed her. She almost closed her eyes waiting for it.

But he smiled briefly, turned and walked down the hall.

She closed the door with a sad sigh. She shouldn't miss the guy who'd been with her in Paris. She hadn't even wanted that kiss. She'd been halfway to her bedroom before he twirled her back. Now she missed him. Missed open, honest, happy Jake.

And she wasn't even entirely sure he existed.

Not wanting to watch more TV, she took out her laptop and searched for *studying for the Pennsylvania bar exam*. Fourteen courses popped up. And that was just the first page.

After twenty minutes of sorting through the entries, her phone rang and, still staring at the computer screen, she answered, "Hello."

"Avery. It's Eileen. I have two people who want to look at the condo tomorrow."

"Really? Already?"

"I told you I had a few clients I knew would be interested. It's not just location. It's that your place is move-in ready. Both of these guys are foreign businessmen who do a lot of work in the city. Both want something simple, no muss, no fuss. I'm bringing one at nine and the other at noon."

"Okay."

She disconnected the call and shifted screens to Jake's text to get his mother's number. After a few pleasantries, she told Maureen that her Realtor had two people coming to look at her condo and asked if she wanted to go shopping the next morning then have lunch.

Maureen said, "Yes! Fantastic! Where would you like to go?"

"You pick," Avery said. After they decided, she hung up the phone and laughed to herself, shaking her head as she walked down the hall. If nothing else had come of the trip to Paris, she had someone she could have lunch with once or twice a week for the next three months.

Unless being with Maureen reminded her of Paris?

She frowned. Thinking about that made her heart skip a beat and swell with longing.

But she could control that...

Couldn't she?

CHAPTER TEN

TWO DAYS LATER, Jake rose from the big chair behind his desk, as his brother and sister entered his office. His secretary had called to announce them, so he wasn't surprised by their arrival. The reason for their visit—as a team—sort of puzzled him though.

As pretty, petite Sabrina sat on the first chair in front of his desk and Seth sat on the other, Jake said, "What's up?"

Sabrina said, "Have you seen Mom lately?"

"Spent three days with her in Paris last week."

"It's all she talks about," Seth said. "How wonderful Avery is and the baby."

"I know. I went to Avery's house Monday night and asked permission for Mom to call her."

"And she said—"

"She said sure. She can't work at Waters, Waters and Montgomery anymore because of conflict of interest. And she doesn't seem predisposed to find another job at six months pregnant. Especially since she needs to study for the Pennsylvania bar exam. I think they'll probably go shopping." He shrugged. "She likes Mom. And Mom adores her." He looked at Seth then Sabrina. "So, what's the problem?"

"Mom's emotionally fragile right now."

"And being with Avery lifts her spirts."

Seth winced. "Yes, but for how long?"

Jake spread his hands in supplication. "About three months. Her doctor is here. She's not moving to Pennsylvania until after the baby is born."

Sabrina's pretty face fell. "She's moving to Pennsylvania?"

"It's where her family lives. That's what studying for the PA bar is all about."

"So, after Mom spends three months doing lunch and shopping with the mother of her first grandchild, Avery's going to Pennsylvania, leaving her alone again?"

Jake scrubbed his hand across his mouth. When Sabrina put it like that, he saw their concerns. "What do you want me to do? Forbid them from seeing each other? Limit the time they spend together?"

Seth quietly said, "How about figuring out

a way to keep her—and Mom's grandchild— *your child*—in New York?"

He squeezed his eyes shut. Seeing Avery on Monday night had been the hardest thing he'd ever done. He'd wanted to chitchat. Make small talk, for God's sake. Hear about her day. He might have made up his mind in Paris that they were a bad match, but on Monday night, the only thing that had kept him from tumbling into the easy familiarity they'd started in Paris was the knowledge that she was his opponent. But even then it was hard. They'd shared too much. Gotten too close. And now he was vulnerable.

He didn't want to convince her to stay. He needed her to go.

"I can't. But even if I could, what if you guys are panicking prematurely? What if three months is enough to bring Mom around? And what if she and Avery form a good enough relationship in that time that Mom's comfortable going to Pennsylvania to visit her grandchild and Avery's comfortable enough to spend weekends with her, here in New York?"

Sabrina sat back in her chair. "It takes a whole year of mourning to get someone through her grief. Mom's only through five months."

"And she'll have three months with Avery

to build the friendship that could take her through the rest of the year and beyond. Avery's a good person." He hadn't realized just how good until they'd spent those days in Paris together. "She and Mom will have a child in common. Enough to form a permanent friendship." He leaned back, fully convinced this was the right thing. "This baby could be just what Mom needs."

Seth drew in a breath and rose. "If Avery stays in New York long enough."

Jake rose too. "The bond may already have formed. The next three months will simply cement it."

Sabrina stood more slowly. "I hope you're right because this works both ways. Getting Mom involved with this woman could break her heart. I saw how Avery ran out of that coffee shop."

Jake winced, remembering that day. Especially how he'd wanted to kiss Avery. But also, how much she'd hated his life, his family's lifestyle. Too big of a dose of that lifestyle could send her packing sooner than she needed to go.

"I'll warn Mom to tread lightly."

When his mother called later that day to gush about lunch with Avery on Tuesday afternoon, he told her not to overwhelm her, but he also realized he had to make sure Avery understood his mom was fragile. After hanging up, he called Avery, but she didn't answer. After two more tries, he left a message on her voice mail that he'd be visiting that night. Though he didn't think it was a good idea for him to see her, his mom was the bigger worry.

At the end of his work day, when every other person employed by McCallan, Inc. had left the floor hours before, he had his driver take him to Avery's apartment building, rode up on the elevator and knocked on her door.

She opened it with a wide smile. "Hey, what are you doing here?"

Her hair was a mess, but her eyes were bright and happy. Memories of their kiss in Paris sizzled through him. He wanted to take her into his arms and kiss her senseless.

"I guess you didn't get my message."

She grinned. "Haven't looked at my phone all day."

Her extreme good mood brought everything back again. Dancing. Laughing. Walking along the Seine in the moonlight.

He should turn. He should run. But he needed to talk to her about his mom. "Can I come in?"

She stepped back so he could enter. "Sure."

The condo smelled like heaven. "Is that spaghetti sauce?"

"My mother's homemade," she said with pride. "And the spaghetti's boiling. I have a big bowl of salad and rolls are in the oven." She smiled at him. "Care to stay for dinner?"

His common sense told him to talk to her about being careful with his mom, maybe limiting their visits, and then race away before his buzzing hormones caused him to cross a line. But his stomach rumbled.

"You can't tell me you're not hungry," she said with a laugh. "And I made way too much." She headed to her kitchen, her steps light, her tone airy. "I now understand why I always ate takeout. Cooking for one is impossible."

He followed her to the bright space with white cabinets, marble countertops and the big, big island made for cooking. Needing the distraction, he ambled around, taking in the perfect kitchen, and almost walked into her when she spun away from the stove.

She caught his shoulders to steady herself. His hands went to her waist to make sure she didn't fall. Their gazes met. Try as he might, he couldn't seem to get his hands to lift off her waist.

His voice was barely a whisper when he said, "I didn't mean to bump into you."

Her eyes darkened with desire that echoed the need billowing through him, making him long to kiss her, to run his hands down her back and maybe through her silky hair.

"It's okay. You were preoccupied with looking around."

Yes. He had been. *Preoccupied.* Not longing to touch her, but studying the room.

The return of rational thought helped him step away from her. "I like your kitchen."

He was glad when she turned and began stirring her sauce. "Meaning you could cook here?"

"Yes."

"I knew I wanted the kitchen to be functional. People notice that when they're searching for a new home. But it also had to be bright and happy." She faced him with a smile. "I think I captured that."

While his entire body was still strung as tight as a violin string, her expression had gone back to normal, as if she wasn't being driven crazy with wanting.

The temptation to kiss her, to remind her of just how good they were together, ripped through him, but common sense and sanity roared back. Paris might have been fun, but it had also been confusing. So many things had happened in those few days, things he normally didn't do, like confide in someone he barely knew. He hadn't thought that through.

Though it had felt good to unburden himself, and the outcome hadn't been bad, he didn't fully understand why he'd gotten so comfortable with her when she could potentially use what he'd told her against him.

He didn't think she would, but the lapse had been perplexing and reminded him that the way they'd been in Paris had been wrong.

Since it was too late to get out of eating with her, he decided light conversation would save him until he could politely race away. "Maybe you should have been a decorator."

"Instead of an attorney?" She laughed. "Remodeling this place was fun. But being a lawyer is more fun. I don't mind going for a jugular now and again. It's good for the soul. Cleansing."

He laughed, but he knew that going for the jugular was her true nature. Not the soft, sweet woman he kept seeing. Not the woman he'd danced with in Paris.

He had to remember that.

"Can I set the table or something?"

She pointed at a cabinet. "Dishes and glasses are up there." She motioned to a drawer above the lower cupboards. "Silverware is there."

He grabbed two plates and the silverware. Paper napkins sat on the table, so he used those. When he returned to the kitchen area, the rolls were in a basket and she was straining the spaghetti.

"The wine's there." She directed him to a wine rack beside bookshelves full of cookbooks.

As he pulled out a bottle, he said, "You must cook a lot more than you admit."

She shook her head. "Nope. All those are my mother's attempt to domesticate me." She brought the spaghetti to the counter. "It'll probably be easier if we bring our dishes out here instead of taking the spaghetti and sauce to the table."

He plucked up the plates and brought both to the big center island. "Ladies first."

"Good. I'm starving."

"I thought you had a big lunch with my mother."

"That was yesterday." She patted her stomach. "But even if it had been today, this child of ours loves to eat."

She filled her plate and walked into the dining area. He filled his, set it on the table then returned to the kitchen for the wine. As he poured himself a glass, he said, "Can I get you some juice?"

"No, but I'd love a bottle of water."

He got her water. Before he took his seat at the table again, he shrugged out of his suit coat, plopped it on the back of his chair and rolled up his sleeves.

When he finally sat, he dug into his spaghetti. Then groaned. "Oh, Lord, that's good. You make me ashamed that I told you I could cook. I don't make anything this delicious."

"It's all about the recipe."

"And timing. And instinct." He glanced over at her. "Don't forget. I might not cook this well, but I cook. I know what goes into it."

Avery held back a sigh. Though what he'd said was complimentary, he delivered it the way a boss talks to an employee. With team spirit that revved up the happy employee being praised, but really didn't touch her.

Her head tilted as she studied him. Same face, same hair, same crystal-blue eyes, but somehow she couldn't see this guy dancing.

She turned her attention to her spaghetti. She missed Paris, but she knew this was for the best. They needed to get along and she didn't "get along" with fun Jake. She wanted to kiss him. She wanted to fall for him. She wanted him to sweep her off her feet—

She experienced a longing so intense she almost sighed again. This was ridiculous. Yearning for something she couldn't have, something that she wasn't even sure existed, was senseless.

Except, he had to exist. She had not imagined what had happened between them in Paris. Several times while walking the streets, dancing, laughing, talking about his father, she'd felt she was dealing with the real Jake.

That's what bothered her. What if *this* guy was the aberration, and Paris Jake was the real one?

Her phone rang, bringing her out of her thoughts. She bounced off her chair. "I have to get this. There were two showings of my house yesterday and both parties were interested. I'm dying to hear if anyone made an offer."

She lifted the phone from the counter, tapped the screen to answer it. "Eileen?"

"Oh, sweetie, do I have good news for you!"

"I got an offer?"

"You got two competing offers. I've been on the phone since three, going back and forth between them. In the end, I got you two hundred thousand more than list price."

She swayed. "What? That's amazing."

"There's just one catch. You have to move out by next week. Both offers were all cash. Both wanted to take possession on Monday."

"Monday! I can't be out on Monday."

"Sure, you can. Let me negotiate the sale

of your furniture with the condo. You hire a mover and pack all your personal items, which will be only a small box truck full of stuff and you're out of there in four days."

The thought of two hundred thousand dollars over asking was too good to pass up. It wasn't as if she was working. She had time to get organized and moved.

"Okay, yes. If the buyer also takes the furniture, I can be out on Monday."

Jake scowled and mouthed, "Monday?"

Eileen said, "Congratulations."

"Thanks." She hung up the phone totally dazed.

"Do not tell me you just agreed to be out of here on Monday."

Still stunned, she fell to the seat across from his. "I had to. Both offers are all cash. Both want the apartment on Monday." She looked over at him. "I should have told her I had nowhere to go. But the offer she wants me to take is two hundred grand over list price." She sucked in a breath. "I thought the asking price was fantastic. I'd have been happy with that...but two hundred thousand dollars more than list?" She shook her head. "I can't turn this down."

"You also can't live on the street."

"I guess I could move to Pennsylvania. Live with my parents until I find a place in Wilton."

"But your doctor is here. You said you were staying for the whole three months."

"I can't if I don't have anywhere to live."

"You can live with me."

She laughed.

When he didn't, she frowned. "Oh. You're serious?"

She pictured a hundred things like eating breakfast together and waiting for him to come home at night and the intimacy of it overwhelmed her. For as much as she'd like the chance to lure Paris Jake back across the Atlantic, she wasn't ready to live with him.

She shook her head. "I don't think so."

He drew a breath, blew it out in a huff. "Okay. So not at my house. How about the family's beach house? It's September. The weather is still warm. And you're not working. Why not enjoy these last few months?"

"If I moved to Pennsylvania I could get a jump on job hunting. I have to take the bar exam, but I'll also need some experience at a firm there."

"Get it after the baby is born. Your doctor is here. My mother loves being part of the pregnancy. You just said yourself you're getting two hundred thousand dollars more than you expected. Take the time off. Relax a bit."

"I shouldn't." But the thought of having

three months of nothing to do but study was very, very tempting. And at a beach house, where she could get some sun, smell the fresh air...

"Okay, if you won't do it for yourself, then do it for me. My mom's been a mess since my dad passed. She came home from Paris talking about you and the baby, just like her old self. You know she's not a stalker or anything. She's looking for something to occupy her."

The way he campaigned for his mom hit her right in the heart. Not because he was kind to his mom but because she suddenly realized how heavy his burden to his family was, and she couldn't say no. It benefitted her, but it also helped him. She'd learned enough about him in Paris to know his life wasn't easy and something inside her couldn't make it more difficult when she could ease his burden by doing something wonderful like live in a beach house.

"Okay."

His eyes widened in disbelief. "Okay?"

She shrugged. "I don't want to leave my doctor and I can study for the bar at a beach house as easily as I can here."

"More easily."

"So, it makes sense."

"Thank you."

Seeing the relief in his eyes, she felt a zing of rightness. Not that she'd done something good. Her decision to stay at his beach house was as much for herself as for him. The sense was more that they'd made a decision together... like a team.

She pulled that thought back, reminding herself that it was dangerous to start liking stiff and formal Jake. He wasn't really a likable guy. He could be. Only a fool would have missed the way his eyes had darkened with desire when he'd bumped into her at the stove. But he'd yanked himself back, because he didn't want to be the guy who melted when they were together.

That was the real bottom line.

He might like her. But he didn't want to. Otherwise, he wouldn't be able to pull back so easily.

Paris Jake was gone. Stuffy Jake was back. It would be dangerous to her heart if she somehow forgot that.

CHAPTER ELEVEN

THE NEXT DAYS passed in a whirl for Avery. The only moving company available on short notice couldn't start until Saturday. But they arrived Saturday morning and immediately began working. Because adding the condo's furnishings into the sale meant she only had to pack personal items, when Maureen surprised her with lunch on Sunday the packing was done and the boxes were already in a truck, waiting to be delivered.

Maureen said, "Well, that's wonderful. We'll drive out to the house right now. We'll eat lunch while your crew unloads the truck, then we can unpack the things you need."

Suspicion tiptoed through Avery's brain. A few weeks ago, the McCallans didn't even know about the pregnancy. Now they were all but running her life. Not only had Jake convinced her to stay and provided a place, but now Maureen was here watching over her.

It had taken the visit from stuffy Jake to remind her the McCallans were accustomed to getting their own way. But she remembered now, and she intended to be very, very careful in dealing not just with Jake, but also with his mother.

"I'm not going to need much help. Jake says there's a room in the back where I can keep all my boxes so I don't have to rent a storage unit."

Maureen slid her arm across Avery's shoulder and directed her to the door. "Considering time for a mortgage, you might want to start looking for your Pennsylvania house now. That way the papers will be signed and it will be yours when you're ready to move."

Taken aback, Avery said, "That's a good idea."

"After I call Jake and tell him to meet us at the beach house with the keys, we can look at listings online on the drive out to the house."

"Okay." Her spirits rose and the little nagging fear that the McCallans were taking over her life began to recede.

Of course, she was paranoid. Stuffy Jake put himself and his family first. Plus, her dad had been bulldozed by people with less money than the McCallans. But as long as they were talking about her moving to Pennsylvania as if it was a done deal, she didn't have anything to worry about...

But she'd keep her guard up.

The drive to Montauk was spent using their phones to look at houses in her small town of Wilton. Maureen seemed to favor Cape Cods, but to Avery the floor plans were too closed off.

When they pulled into the driveway of the beach house, Avery looked up and saw the enormous home and she blinked, wondering how Maureen could have seen good in any of the houses they'd researched online. Compared to this beast even the big Colonial they'd considered had been tiny.

They got out of the limo and Avery stared at the monstrosity before her. Three stories of stone with huge windows and brown shutters, the house could have been a castle for Britain's royal family.

She said, "Wow."

Jake strode toward them, bouncing a set of keys in his hand. Dressed in jeans and a T-shirt, with his hair sexily tumbled and a day's growth of beard on his chin and cheeks, he looked like Paris Jake. Memories came back swift and sure, first Jake standing by the window, unshaven with his hair wild, looking like he hadn't slept; then the kiss, the way he'd taken possession, emotionally, sexily.

She blinked, trying to force the images away but they wouldn't leave.

"I thought the plan was to move tomorrow?"

"Everything was packed," Avery said, working not to stutter over how good he looked or the wonderful memories. "No point in waiting."

"We've brought lunch," Maureen said, displaying her bags of Chinese food. "Eat with us then you can show Avery everything she needs to know about the house."

She'd rather he left. She liked Paris Jake a little too much and she didn't want to start superimposing his characteristics on real Jake the way she had when she showed the condo to Eileen.

He unlocked the door to a foyer so big and so empty, their footsteps echoed around them as they walked through to the kitchen in the back. Three French doors stood side by side, providing a heart-stopping view of the ocean.

"Oh, my God."

Maureen walked up behind her. "I know. It's lovely, isn't it?"

"It's spectacular," Jake agreed. "Wait until you see it from the third floor. I'll take you around after we eat."

She didn't want to go any farther into the house than she had to. She didn't want to see Jake looking like he did in Paris and acting like a stranger, but more than that she only needed a bathroom, bedroom and kitchen.

She glanced around. The size of the place was simply overwhelming. Not comfortable, not cozy. She didn't want to insult Jake or his mom but she had no idea how someone relaxed here.

In the airy white kitchen with three ovens and two refrigerators, they heated the Chinese food Maureen had brought and ate at a table with an ocean view. Then they took a quick tour of the downstairs, through a formal dining room, a library, an entertainment room and three sitting rooms, one of which faced the ocean. Jake opened the wall-sized door that folded until the space blended into the enormous patio behind it.

The heat of the day raced into the room, bringing with it the salty scent of the water, reminding her of vacations before her dad was arrested. The beach had been her favorite place back then.

"It's amazing."

For the first time ever, she could see her child fitting into the McCallans' life. Not the limos, penthouses and mansions part, but the big yard and the beach. She could see a little girl in a pink ruffled-rump bathing suit making a sandcastle on the private stretch of ocean beyond the big grassy back yard, or a little boy running up to the waves, dangling his toes in the water and giggling as he ran out again.

Maureen sighed dreamily. "It's the perfect summer retreat."

Looking past the long stretch of grass at the blue water, Avery could see that.

Maureen brushed her hands off as if she'd done her work for the day then turned to Avery. "I'm going to let you alone. Give you some time to get settled." She leaned in and kissed her cheek. "I'll call you Tuesday. No pressure if you're busy studying."

When the front door closed behind Maureen, the room filled with awkward silence. Except this time, with the thoughts of her child vacationing in this house running through her head, Avery's heart squeezed. All this time she'd been thinking about her feelings for Jake and the way he treated her and she'd missed the obvious. This stiff, formal man was her child's father. Avery might move on, but her child had to deal with this Jake forever.

"Are you ready to see the upstairs?"

She looked at him, remembered him funny and silly in Paris and knew *that* Jake would make a much better dad.

"Sure."

With Jake leading, they climbed the circular stairway in the foyer. It twisted in such a way that they passed the second-floor windows at the same time his mom's limo drove off.

He stopped and faced her. "I totally forgot about your car. Driving out with my mom means you left your car behind in the city."

"I don't own a car."

"How do you get to work?" He frowned. "You take the subway?"

He said *subway* as if her using it was a crime. "It's not poison and it's really convenient. And cheap." Once again, she worried for their child. Not that he'd be hurt or kidnapped because of the McCallans, but that he'd get a skewed perspective of life. "It costs a small fortune for parking downtown, and renting a parking space in my building would kill my monthly budget."

"Sorry." He shook his head. "Got it."

He walked by the first bedroom and the second, but stopped at the third and opened the door on a room large enough to have two reading chairs by a bay window, a king bed and two dressers.

"We can bring up a box or two of your clothes and unpack if you like."

Seeing the room, she relaxed, but only a bit. All of her worst visions about her child's time with Jake ran through her head and she wanted some time alone to think this through. "No. I'm fine. I can get them myself."

Jake sighed, not wanting to offend her, but wondering if her lifting boxes and carrying them up a flight of stairs was a good idea. "You're sure."

"If I have to take the clothes out of the box one shirt at a time, that's what I'll do."

"Okay." Now she was the beleaguered peasant and he was Marie Antoinette again. She'd taken his comment about the subway all wrong and suddenly she hated him.

They might not become best friends, but after her doing him the favor of staying in New York, he didn't like the idea that they had to be enemies either.

But could people be opponents without being enemies?

His father would argue they couldn't, but it didn't seem right to be enemies when she was helping him. Plus, he'd spent his life working not to be like his dad. Maybe this was one of those things he should consider changing?

As they walked down the stairs, he got a call from one of his vice presidents. Scuttlebutt had it that a bid they'd submitted was millions of dollars higher than the closest competitor.

At the bottom of the steps, he motioned to Avery that he would be going into the library to talk to Bill Cummings. She nodded and headed for the back of the house, where the movers had stashed her boxes.

Immersed in the discussion, he sank into a thick leather chair behind a French provincial desk and for two hours debated the wisdom and feasibility of changing their bid.

His call completed, he spent five minutes looking for Avery, then realized she was probably in her room, maybe showering or napping after the long day.

He didn't want to leave without saying goodbye, and making peace, but he also didn't want to go up to her room.

He returned to the library, turned on the computer and located the bid to go over the numbers one more time.

She ambled into the library over an hour later, looking as she had when she awoke from her naps in Paris. Hair tousled. Eyes sleepy and sexy.

His breath caught. His heart softened. She was the sexiest woman he'd ever met and recently he'd been realizing she was also the kindest. He refused to let his dad's antiquated ideas hurt her anymore. He just wasn't sure how to change things. "You were sleeping."

"I thought you'd left, but when I went into the kitchen to make a sandwich, I saw your car."

He rose from behind the desk. "I didn't want to leave without saying goodbye." And making peace, but what would he say? *I'm sorry I'm rich? I'm sorry I want to see my child a little more than I think you're going to let me?*

She smiled. "Thanks."

That smile did things to him he would never understand. He longed to run his fingers through her rumpled hair, maybe tilt her chin up for a kiss.

And that was another problem.

He had to work out how they'd handle their attraction if they were to remain friends. He'd seen what had happened in Paris. When they mixed getting along with their attraction, he'd kissed her, confided things he should have kept to himself.

Maybe it would be better to leave and think this through before he offered an olive branch.

He motioned for her to walk out with him. "Since you're fine and set up, I'll be going."

She yawned. "I'll probably get a shower and go back to bed."

"Sounds great."

A strange feeling settled over him, the way it had when they'd walked side by side in Paris and she wouldn't let him hold her hand or put his arm across her shoulders. Awkward didn't describe it. Neither did uncomfortable. It was more like melancholy. But it wasn't coming from him. It was coming from her.

She stayed at the front door as he walked to his car. Once he was inside, she inched backward into the house, closing the door behind her.

He put the car in gear and headed along the circular driveway, but his thoughts stayed on Avery. She was a normally happy woman. But today she'd been off. He'd thought she was angry, but what if she'd been sad?

He wished he was the kind of guy who could go back and ask her. But what would he say? "You looked sad. It made me feel awful."

That was going beyond offering an olive branch and making peace.

Besides, she'd think he was crazy.

He was an hour into the drive when their conversation about her taking the subway replayed in his head and he realized she didn't have a car. Not only had he taken her to a huge house that made her uneasy, he'd stranded her there.

Now *that* was a reason to go back.

He turned around at the first opportunity and headed to the beach house. By the time he arrived, it was dark. Not one light shone in the rows of windows in the three-story stone giant. He blew his breath out then ambled up the sidewalk to the front door.

He opened it into darkness, recognizing he wasn't going to get a chance to talk to her. He tossed his keys on an available table, then decided Avery probably wouldn't find them there. Even if he left a note explaining that he was giving her the use of his car, it would do her no good if she didn't find the note or the keys.

Walking into the kitchen, he turned on the light, found a pen and paper and wrote a note explaining that he was leaving the house key and the keys to his car, which was parked in the driveway.

When he was done, he shook his head. He should have called his driver first. Actually, he should have called his driver on the way back to Montauk. But he hadn't.

Now it was late.

Texting Gerry, he headed up the hidden stairway in the back of the butler's pantry.

Pick me up at the beach house tomorrow morning around nine.

It looked like he'd get a chance to talk to her after all.

The next morning, Avery awakened with a start, her heart pounding, her breath coming in shaky gasps. She looked around, remembered she was staying at the McCallan beach house and rolled out of bed.

She'd get accustomed to the emptiness of the huge, cavernous house. She would. She had to.

She brushed her teeth, washed her face and tiptoed into the silent hallway. It was like being alone in a hotel. The vacant corridor echoed with her footsteps. So why did she have the ungodly feeling she wasn't alone? That someone was following her?

She swore she heard a noise. A faint sound. Like somebody dropping something.

She picked up the pace, racing down the big circular stairway to the foyer, her thin robe billowing behind her, telling herself not to jump to conclusions. If there was somebody else in the house it was undoubtedly a maid. Or gardener. Or somebody else employed by the McCallans.

She should calm down.

Just because she was in a huge mansion she didn't know, stuck here unless she called a taxi, that didn't mean something sinister would happen. As for that feeling that she wasn't alone—she'd already figured out it was probably a maid.

She pushed open the door to the kitchen and stopped dead in her tracks. She was not imagining the scent of toast. She sniffed the air... or was that bagels?

"Good morning."

Her heart tumbled. *Jake.*

"What are you doing here?"

He motioned her to the table with the view of the ocean. "I made bagels."

Confused, she walked over and took a seat, her traitorous heart knocking against her ribs. Had he realized how uncomfortable she was and come back the night before to protect her? If he had, it was about the sweetest thing he'd ever done. "Thanks."

Setting two bagels on the table, he sat across from her. "You're welcome."

He was dressed in the same clothes he'd worn the day before, though the scruffy beard was gone...*because it was Monday.* "Shouldn't you be at work?"

"I'm getting there. My driver will be here at nine."

Maybe he hadn't come back for her, but because his car had broken down? "What happened to your car?"

"Nothing. I was an hour into the drive home last night before I realized we'd left you here without transportation." He shrugged. "You could have called one of our drivers, but I figured you'd rather have access to a car. So I'm leaving the Porsche."

He had come back because he'd recognized she was uncomfortable.

Her heart warmed. Her pulse fluttered.

"Anyway, when I realized we'd stranded you, I drove back. You were already asleep, and I didn't bother you." He shrugged again. "Or my driver. Nobody wants a Sunday night call, telling them to drive out to the beach to pick up their boss. Especially when it was just as easy for me to stay."

She stared at him. This was Paris Jake coming out and he didn't even realize it. She wondered if he knew he was thinking about her, putting her first, then the baby kicked.

She grabbed her stomach. "Oh, ouch! That was a good one."

His face lit up. "The baby?"

"Yes."

He wanted to touch the baby. She could see it in his expression. But he wouldn't ask.

She laughed. "Come here. I know you want to feel him."

He eased out of his chair and walked over cautiously. When he reached her, he stooped down to be eye level with her belly and put his hands on either side of the baby bump the way she'd taught him in Paris.

The baby didn't kick this time. It did a full-on stretch and roll.

His gaze jumped to hers. "He totally changed positions."

She should have been uncomfortable with his hands on her so intimately, but the shine in his eyes stopped that in its tracks. This was the guy she wanted to be her baby's father. The unguarded man who simply reacted, didn't think everything through.

"He probably gets tired of being in one spot all the time."

The baby tumbled again and Jake laughed. "Cramped quarters."

The happiness in his voice made her heart swell. He loved this baby. It was weird to think she'd ever believed he'd be happier not knowing he was a father. But her fears from the day before weren't unfounded. This guy would make a great dad. The stuffy guy? Not so much. And come hell or high water, she had to teach him to be himself with their baby.

She tried a joke. "Too bad I can't give him one of the ten bedrooms upstairs."

He winced. "You took a tour?"

"No. I just counted doors in the hall and figured there had to be at least two more bedrooms on the third floor."

"We usually have a lot of guests here. Especially after our Christmas ball."

She rolled her eyes. "I'll bet it's a blast."

"It is." His words weren't sharp, but they were defensive.

Hating the way she'd ruined what could have been a very nice moment, she batted her hand. "Don't mind me. I've got to get studying today and I don't really feel like it."

The baby stopped moving and Jake rose. "Then don't study. Take a walk on the beach."

She gaped at him. "Have you seen the walk *to* the beach?"

"It's just beyond the yard."

"The yard is the size of a football field. Someday when I'm in the mood for serious exercise I'll tackle that."

His phone pinged and Jake grabbed it from the table. "It's my driver." He glanced around uneasily. "Are you going to be okay here?"

"Sure. Yes." She smiled, forcing herself not to look ungrateful. She loved when he behaved informally, kind, ready to be a father.

She wished she could figure out a way to have him act that way all the time.

He tucked his phone in his pocket and turned to her. For thirty seconds, Avery thought he was going to kiss her. Not a heart-stirring, heart-stopping kiss like they'd shared in Paris, but a goodbye kiss. The way he once would have kissed her when she was racing out the door of his penthouse.

Their gazes met before he quickly turned away.

But that almost kiss cemented her feelings. Jake was changing. That guy she met in Paris? That was the real Jake. And not only would he make a great dad, but Avery wasn't just crazy about him. She could trust him.

And that was a problem.

Was it smart to trust him when she wasn't really sure the changes would last?

CHAPTER TWELVE

SHE HATED THE HOUSE.

Jake wasn't letting his mind go there to get his thoughts off the way he'd almost slipped and brushed a quick kiss across her lips before he left. The almost kiss had been an aberration. The way she didn't like the house was a fact.

If they were going to get along, he had to do something about the house.

He arrived at the office, still antsy about Avery being unhappy, but when he bumped into Seth in the hall on his way to his office, the answer hit him.

"Do you and your friends still have that little beach house in Montauk?"

Seth said, "You mean the one down the road from the family house?"

"Yes."

"We have it, but we don't use it as much now that Clark married Harper and Oz and Tina live together."

"Good. I need it."

Seth laughed. "You need it?"

"Avery's condo sold. I invited her to live in the family house and she hates it."

Seth's eyes narrowed. "Hates it? How can she hate it?"

"It's big and she's alone. I know she'd be happier in your bungalow if you don't mind."

"Sure. It's better to have someone staying there than leaving the place empty."

"She'll be there until the baby's born... If that's okay."

"I told you. We don't use it as much as when we could leave work early on Fridays, drive up and drink beer for three days." He sighed. "I miss that."

Jake remembered having to drive to Montauk to bail him, Clark and Oz out of jail. "I don't."

Seth only laughed. "I'll get you the keys to the place when I go to lunch."

Seth started down the hall but Jake called after him, "It's clean, isn't it?"

Without turning around Seth called, "We have a service come in after anyone uses it."

Jake's spirits lifted. He pulled out his phone to call Avery but decided he liked surprising her. When Seth brought the keys to him after lunch, Jake told his administrative assistant he would be working in the car the rest of the day and took the limo back to his apartment to change into jeans and a T-shirt, then told Gerry to drive him to the Montauk house.

He didn't question why he'd changed clothes. Avery seemed to be more comfortable with him when he wasn't in a suit. And he, well, he liked being comfortable. They were going to a bungalow beach house, something that virtually sat in the sand. Being in jeans and a T-shirt and tennis shoes was simply smarter.

Opening the door of the family house, he called, "Anybody home?"

"In the kitchen."

He followed the sound of Avery's voice and found her making a peanut-butter-and-jelly sandwich. "I hope that's not your dinner."

She stared at him for a few seconds. Her gaze took a stroll down his T-shirt and jeans and she smiled. "Why? Peanut butter has lots of protein and raspberry jelly's just plain good."

His body reacted the way it always did when she looked at him. His heart rate picked up. His muscles tightened. It took every ounce of discipline he could muster not to walk over and kiss her.

"Because it's almost four and you need a vegetable."

She laughed. "I get plenty of those. This is a snack." She took her sandwich from the counter and dropped it on a little plate. "So, what's up? Why are you here?"

"I have a surprise."

She smiled again, as if totally thrilled. "You do?"

This smile washed through him like much-needed summer rain. The attraction was a complication but her liking things he did for her was right. Good.

"Yes. My brother owns a beach house with two friends. It was something they bought to spend weekends out of the city when their investment firm took off. Anyway, they barely use it anymore since his two friends have settled down, and I asked if you could stay there a few months."

"You're moving me?"

He held out his hand. "Come with me to see it and if you don't like it, you can stay here."

She displayed her plate with the peanut-butter-and-jelly sandwich on it. "Can I bring this?"

He laughed. "Sure."

He snagged the Porsche keys from the center island and led her outside to his car. "I'll tell Gerry to wait for us."

Her head tilted. "Won't he be bored?"

"He's taking classes a few nights a week. When I'm gone for stretches like this he studies. Trust me, I'm not abusing him."

She winced. "Sorry."

"That's okay. I'd rather you bring up things like this than hate me in silence."

She muttered, "I don't hate you," as she rounded the car hood to the passenger seat.

Warm relief filled him, until he realized he knew that. It wasn't him she disliked but his lifestyle. Moving her to a comfortable home fixed that. He was so proud of himself he tossed the keys in the air before he opened the Porsche door and slid inside.

The drive to Seth's beach house took ten minutes. The second Avery saw the bungalow, her eyes lit.

"Oh, my gosh."

Aqua with white shutters and a white stone walkway to the navy blue front door, the little house all but said peace and tranquility.

She shoved open her car door and raced up the walkway, Jake on her heels.

She couldn't get in fast enough after he opened the door. A tan sofa and two chairs sat on a fluffy beige rug that covered hardwood floors. Multicolored throw pillows and bright orange curtains broke up the monotony of all the browns. Beyond the living area was a white kitchen that had two sets of French doors that showcased the ocean that wasn't even as far away as the walk across the backyard at the family house.

"It's perfect."

He bounced the keys in his hand, enjoying his pride at pleasing her. "There are three bedrooms and three baths." He pointed out the French doors. "And as you can see, the deck is huge."

She nodded eagerly, motioning to the big white dining table beside the kitchen. "And I can study there." She turned to him with a smile. "You didn't have to do this."

"I know." He drew in a quick breath. "I hated seeing you uncomfortable."

"Thanks." She laughed and impulsively hugged him.

He squeezed his eyes shut as happiness filled him. The kind he rarely felt. Their baby brushed his stomach and the rightness of the moment about swept him away.

He did hate seeing her uneasy, but there was more to it than that. More to it than responsibility. He had this odd feeling that this was his place. With her. And the more she liked the things he did for her, the more he wanted to do.

They were no longer enemies.

But they were still opponents.

His thoughts from Paris came tumbling back. That getting along meant losing control. *You can't be an equal. Always negotiate from a position of strength.*

His heart stilled as his dad's words echoed in his brain. He'd always believed that was one of the things his father had gotten right. And he still believed negotiating from a position of strength was good for business. But what if it was the wrong thing for him personally?

And what if that was his real problem? The way his dad had treated him had turned him into a crafty businessman. Someone even able to take down his father when the time was right. But it hadn't taught him a damn thing about being a dad or having any sort of personal relationship at all.

That's what really had been troubling him since Avery told him she was pregnant. He didn't know how to be a parent, let alone a good father, but the truth went deeper. He didn't know how to have a personal life.

The conclusion was so striking he almost needed to sit. She'd called him stuffy. But he wasn't stuffy. He just always held himself at a distance. It made life easier. Less complicated.

He'd learned that from dealing with his dad. Keep him at arm's distance, while keeping the relationship equitable. Get comfortable and he'd snatch the rug out from under you.

But Avery wasn't his dad.

She was smart, beautiful, the mother of his child and their encounters had gone from sexual to adversarial to…personal. She was picking her way along the same way he was. Adjusting to having him in her life. But she was doing it a hell of a lot more honestly than he was.

All this time he'd thought he was protecting himself, when maybe he simply didn't know how to let go.

He pulled himself out of Avery's hug. "We should go get your stuff."

She headed to the door. "Great."

He drove them back to the mansion and she bounced out of the car like an eager kid at Christmas.

"I only took one suitcase of clothes upstairs to my room. Let me repack that and I'll be good to go."

"You don't want the other things?"

"Not for right now. I'd like to leave most of the boxes stored in your back room, if you don't mind."

"Okay. You're the one who'll be living with next to nothing."

"I'm fine with that. Jeans, a few shirts, some pajamas and I'm good."

They walked into the foyer and she raced up the stairs to pack. Ten minutes later, she arrived at the top of the steps with a duffel bag big enough to hold a body.

"Don't you carry that!"

He ran up the stairs and caught the handle of the duffel, so he could take it down the stairs. "No wonder you said you only needed one suitcase."

"Hey, there's a hair dryer and curling iron and cosmetics in there too."

"Oh, well, that explains it."

He managed to get the thing in the trunk of his Porsche, though just barely. They drove to Seth's beach house and once again she hurried out. As they headed up the sidewalk, with him carrying her duffel bag, she took the keys from his hand and opened the door for him.

She made a small production number out of choosing her room, then he tossed the duffel bag onto the bed. He expected her to dismiss him so she could unpack; instead she turned to him.

"Let's take a walk on the beach."

He hadn't intended to—

Or had he? He glanced down at his T-shirt, jeans and tennis shoes and wondered if his subconscious hadn't planned this all along.

If he was going to be fair and honest, the

way she was, maybe it was time to go with his feelings.

"A walk on the beach sounds great."

They stepped out onto the back deck and she locked the French doors then pocketed the keys.

This time, he didn't debate holding her hand and she didn't fight it. They strolled down to the water. When they reached it, she took in a long drink of air and sighed.

"Now, this is a beach house."

She turned them to the left and began walking along the shore, a few feet from the wet mark left by the last high wave. Warm sun beat down on them. The sound of the surf became background music.

"My family and I used to go to Virginia Beach."

The stiffness of his chest loosened a bit. Now that he wasn't fighting his feelings, he saw the comment for what it was. She was telling him things about her life again, continuing the process of getting to know each other.

"Oh, yeah?"

"I have a brother. He's a year older than I am." She peeked at him. "He's a firefighter."

"No kidding."

"He's not a thrill seeker. He likes helping people."

"Must run in the family." He wanted to ask why her brother hadn't been the one to go to school, to sacrifice his life to make up for the fact that there had been no one to help her dad, but he stayed quiet.

"We're not nuts."

"I know."

"In a way, we're sort of like you. You give money to help people. We use our careers."

"Makes sense." He supposed it did, except it rubbed him all the wrong ways that she'd had a dream of working and living in New York and she'd abandoned it.

Still, when they returned to the bungalow an hour later and he stepped into the cozy house, he supposed there were different kinds of comforts in the world. This was a house a person could relax in. He could see himself cooking in the kitchen, watching a football game on the big screen in the living room, as Avery studied at the long dining table.

And for the first time since he'd met her, he wondered if they didn't actually belong together.

Avery had never had such a good time. Jake really was becoming a different person, and she and the baby were part of it.

But they needed more time. God knew when

he'd visit again. She had to make the best use of every minute she had with him.

As she closed the door, she said, "I'd cook you supper, but we don't have any food here."

He winced. "Sorry, I should have thought of that."

"There's a market up the street."

"You've been there?"

"I took a spin in your pretty black Porsche." She grinned at him. "It's not every day a girl gets a sports car left at her disposal."

He laughed and pulled the car keys from his pocket. "Let's go."

Settling behind the steering wheel as she buckled her seat belt, he asked, "What do you want to eat?"

"A big juicy steak." She rubbed her hands together. "I saw the grill on the deck. We can get some veggies and makings for a salad and have a feast."

"Sounds like a good idea." Before he shifted into Reverse to get them on the road, he pulled out his phone. He clicked a few buttons then said, "Hey, it looks like I'm going to be here at least another three hours. If there's anything you want to do, go. I'll call you when I'm ready."

He hung up the phone and glanced at her. "See? I take care of my people."

She wished she hadn't been so critical of him, then realized this might be a good time to show him she could change too. "I know. I've seen it before. I'm sorry for being judgmental."

He grinned. "Well, what do you know? Another apology."

She laughed. "Just drive."

It took them twenty minutes to find the store. Coming at it from a different direction, Avery lost her way twice. Jake laughed at her, then used his phone app to find the store the easy way.

They picked up steaks, veggies, things for salad, pickles, peanut butter and jelly, and Avery had a good time laughing at the way he gasped at the prices. He'd shopped, of course, while at the university, but not recently. He also seemed to love her strange cravings.

At the checkout he let her pay half. Another sign that he'd been paying attention when she talked. She teased him that he was paying for that night's dinner and she took care of the milk, juice, four different kinds of cookies, bread, eggs, peanut butter, jelly, hamburger meat and pickles.

"That'll keep me until tomorrow."

Sliding into the driver's seat, he cut her a sideways glance. "Seriously."

"I'm kidding."

He gave her a doubtful look and appeared to be about to tease her, but his phone rang. He slid it from his pants pocket and tossed it to Avery. "Answer that."

She glanced down at the caller ID. "It's your mom."

"Put it on speaker."

When she pressed the button, he said, "Hey, Mom."

"Jake, oh, Jake. I can't find Seth!"

Wincing at his mom's melodrama, he said, "Is he lost?"

"Clark was killed in an automobile accident this afternoon."

Jake instantly pulled the Porsche into a convenience store parking lot to give his mother his full attention. "Say that again?"

"Seth's partner Clark was killed today." Maureen burst into tears. "I'm reeling. And if I am this upset I can only imagine how bad Seth is. Sabrina went to his apartment. He's not there."

Avery watched fear race across Jake's face. "I have an idea or two of where he could be. I'll find him."

"Let me know the minute you do."

Avery disconnected the call as Jake shoved the gearshift into Reverse and laid rubber pulling out of the convenience store. "I'll take you home. We'll get the food inside," he said as he sent the car screaming down the quiet street of the lovely beach town. But when he looked over at her, his gaze dipped to her stomach and he slowed his pace.

He drove carefully down the streets to Seth's bungalow. When they got there, he helped her carry her groceries inside and even put the perishables in her fridge.

Then he headed for the door and she followed him.

"Where do you think you're going?"

"With you." He was so upset his driving couldn't be trusted. But he seemed to restrain himself when she was in the car. Maybe to protect his child? Maybe to protect her? Whatever the reason, she wouldn't let him go alone. Not now. Not when their feelings for each other were growing and changing and potentially becoming something wonderful.

"I'm not letting you drive by yourself like this."

"I'm fine."

"Good, then we'll just have a nice trip into the city together."

"It's late and you're tired."

She pushed him toward the door. "Oh, crazy, crazy man. I've told you. I'm pregnant.

Not sick. Now get a move on or I'll grab the keys and drive."

That threat was enough to get him walking again. Inside the car, he started the engine and headed to the city.

She kept him talking, first just small talk, then when he seemed calm, she segued into asking about Seth's friend.

"They just found out Clark's wife Harper is pregnant."

"Oh." *Oh, Lord.* She began to understand his anxiety. He knew Clark's child wouldn't have a dad and it affected him differently than it would have before he'd learned he was going to become a father himself.

The almost three-hour drive seemed never ending, but eventually they made it into the city. After trying Seth's cell phone again and again, they stopped at his apartment. Jake had a key. He didn't knock. He opened the door and walked inside, but Seth wasn't there.

Sitting on the sofa, he pulled out his phone. Avery sat beside him.

"I have the number for Clark's parents. I didn't want to have to bother them, but if he's there with them—"

He broke off as he hit the Contacts button. After a few seconds he said, "Hello, this is Jake McCallan, there's no need to disturb the

Hargraves." Avery assumed he was either talking to a maid or someone who'd gone to their house to comfort Clark's parents. "I'm just calling to see if my brother Seth is there." A pause. "He isn't? You're sure?" He closed his eyes. "Thank you."

He disconnected the call. "Okay, so next is the apartment of an old girlfriend."

"You can't call?"

"I don't have her number. I only know her address because they had a party there once." He combed his fingers through his hair. "Seth believes Clark saved him. He was this blue-collar kid, scraping by, but he took Seth in when Seth dropped off the grid because of our dad. Clark didn't expect any money—not even rent—he just took him in."

The unexpected confidence filled her heart with both joy and sorrow. It was wonderful that he knew he could turn to her. Heartrending that he had to.

"People who don't have money can be very generous."

"Seth paid him back by giving him half of the investment firm without any up-front capital." He shook his head again. "They lived in their dodgy apartment for the next five years, long after each could have afforded his own place." His eyes closed. "This will have hit

Seth too hard to comprehend. I know he considers Clark more of a brother than he does me."

Avery rubbed her hand across his shoulders. "Hey. When you needed him, Seth left his investment firm to take a place in your company. You're brothers."

He blew his breath out on a sigh. "Yes. We are." He rose and extended his hand to help Avery stand. "Let's go find him."

Seth wasn't at his last girlfriend's. He wasn't at any of the hangouts he frequented. Desperate, Jake drove to the neighborhood where Seth had lived with Clark and Oz.

Avery's heart nearly exploded with relief when Jake said, "There's his car."

They parked on the street five cars behind Seth's. As they approached the Cadillac SUV, they could see Seth behind the wheel, leaning back on the seat as if he was sleeping.

Jake knocked on the window and Seth's head snapped up. "Open the window."

Seth opened the door. "What? What do you want?" He looked around. "What time is it?"

"It's after midnight."

Avery hugged her arms around herself, warding off the chilly night air. "We're here to take you home."

Seth rubbed his hand down his face. "You heard about Clark?"

"Mom called."

Seth closed his eyes, obviously struggling to control his emotions.

Avery's heart broke for Seth, but she saw Jake's strength. He wouldn't let Seth go through this alone. He wasn't just the leader of his family; he loved his brother. Made allowances. Didn't cast aspersions or point fingers.

Jake said, "Avery will drive your car back to your place and I'll drive you."

Avery noticed the empty liquor bottle beside Seth in the passenger seat. Understanding why Jake wanted her to drive, she held back a wince, and as playfully as possible said, "I've always wanted to drive a Caddy."

Seth sucked in a long breath. "This is wrong."

Jake reached in and undid his seatbelt. "Yeah, I know."

"He wasn't even thirty."

Sliding the shoulder harness down his arms, Jake helped him out of the SUV. "You told me he was a year or two younger."

"And Harper's pregnant."

"I know. We talked about it last week."

Avery helped Jake walk Seth to the Porsche then quickly opened the door. They got him into the passenger's seat and buckled in, then Jake reminded her of the address to Seth's apartment. She put it into her phone GPS just in case she lost Jake as they were returning to Seth's.

After a twenty-minute drive, it took ten minutes to find a parking space on the street and another ten to get Seth upstairs and onto his bed, face-first, in his clothes.

When they walked into the sitting area, Jake said, "I'm not sure if he's passed out or sleeping."

"It probably doesn't matter."

"I called my mom while we were driving here to let her know Seth was safe." He dug into his pocket and produced the Porsche keys. "Here, take these. I'm staying." As soon as the words were out of his mouth, he shook his head. "Actually, it's awfully late for you to be making an almost three-hour drive back to the beach house."

She yawned.

"You're staying too." He pointed back to the hall. "Seth has a spare bedroom. I'll sleep on the sofa."

That seemed absolutely stupid, considering their past.

And their present.

They were having a baby. He'd kissed her in

Paris and almost kissed her at least three times since they'd returned. She liked him—might even love him. She'd never stopped her merry-go-round of work long enough to really get to know anyone to love them. Yet, it seemed fate had set things up with Jake so she'd not only have time, she'd have ways to get to know him. Not just as a boyfriend or lover but as a wonderful human being.

She caught his hand. "Are you daft? Not only have we slept together often enough that it's ridiculous to be splitting hairs, but I like you." She caught his gaze. "And you like me."

His eyes stayed locked with hers. "I do."

Light burst inside her. He liked her, but more than that, two weeks ago he never would have been able to make the admission.

But neither would she.

She turned him in the direction of the hall. "Go."

They walked to the bedroom and found extra toothbrushes in the guest bathroom. After stripping down to T-shirts and underwear, they climbed into bed.

Instinct and need rattled through her. The urge to nestle against him trembled along her skin. But it was late and she was tired. She would bet he was too.

Still, she didn't roll away. She lay unmoving

beside him, half hoping he would turn and kiss her. For some reason, she couldn't kiss him. Probably because she'd been the one to break the ice and admit she liked him, and force him to admit he liked her too.

He had to make the next move.

She yawned. The warmth of his body spread into the covers and over to her. She closed her eyes and let it take away the chill that had seeped into her bones while they stood on the street with Seth.

CHAPTER THIRTEEN

AVERY FELL ASLEEP almost instantly and Jake closed his eyes, savoring her nearness and the fact that they'd said what they'd both been thinking.

They liked each other.

He'd thought they were opposites, but the more he got to know her the more he realized they shared work ethic, love of family, a desire to do something good in the world.

A few weeks in each other's company had shown them the obvious. They were more alike than they were different.

He'd always believed it would be frightening to be so vulnerable, but every time he thought of having her in his life there was a tightness in his chest that was more anticipation of joy than fear.

The thought kept him awake for another hour. Things might not work out and she could leave him. They could still fight. They hadn't settled the logistics of their lives...a million things could happen.

But he didn't give in to fear. Never had. Never would. He took action. He could control so many of the things that might bedevil them. He would focus on those.

Confident, he drifted off.

Hours later, he woke with a start. He would have bounced up in bed, except something held him in place. He glanced down and found Avery nestled into his side. Her head on his shoulder like a pillow.

His heart expanded as the events of the day before came back to him. They'd walked on the beach, shopped, found Seth together. But all those were quickly overshadowed by how damned wonderful she felt snuggled against him.

He enjoyed the feeling for a minute or two, then slid out of bed to use the bathroom and brush his teeth. When he returned she was awake, sitting up on the bed with all her glorious red hair a tumbled mess flowing around her.

"Good morning."

It took a second before he found his voice. They weren't just a hookup anymore. They liked each other. She was beautiful, smart, kind. And his for the taking.

"Good morning."

She got out of bed before he had a chance to get back in. Disappointment roared through him. "Where are you going?"

"There's a little person on my bladder. Never question a pregnant woman on her way to the bathroom." She rose to her tiptoes and brushed a quick kiss across his lips. Her eyes filled with promise. "Get back in bed."

He laughed lightly as she scampered past him, though his heart thudded in his chest. Everything was so different between them now. Better.

She returned a few minutes later, slid under the covers and nestled against him.

"I wonder if Seth is up."

Her voice was soft, a low, quiet whisper, because if Seth was still sleeping, she wouldn't want to wake him. Now that they had spent time together, real time, doing normal things, he knew that about her. He knew she was good. She knew he wasn't stuffy as much as responsible.

She was the first person ever to really know him. The first person to ever really care to know him. And she'd come back to bed, because this was right.

"I doubt he's awake yet."

"I don't hear anything beyond the door."

Jake shrugged, feeling her silky hair move against his skin, waking all his nerve endings.

"He's going to need fluids, aspirin and something to eat."

"If he drank that whole bottle of whiskey, the something to eat might have to wait until about noon or so."

She shifted against him. "I wonder what time it is."

He leaned over and got his phone from the bedside table. "A little after seven."

"We should get up. Check on Seth."

He realized she was stalling. Maybe waiting for him to make the first move. "Or we could stay here."

She laughed, low and throaty. "Why, Mr. McCallan. Are you propositioning me?"

She knew damned well he was, but he liked the flirting. He liked being reminded of how they had been when they met, as much as he liked how their relationship had morphed into something more.

He pulled back, smoothed his hand along her tummy, feeling the child that would bring them together before he let it skim down her hips, along her thighs and back up again.

She sighed with contentment, and he bent down, pressed his mouth to hers, starting slowly, enjoying her plump lips, then he deepened the kiss as she rolled to her side.

He could have ravaged her. That's what his hormones ached to do. It's also what he would have done six months ago. But this was no longer about having sex. This was about emotion.

He liked her.

And she liked him.

The sheer joy of it filled him as a horrible retching noise rent the air.

Avery's eyes popped open. "Oh-oh."

Jake sighed.

"We should go and help him."

He nuzzled her neck. "He's a grown man. He'll be fine."

"Um, Jake. If we can hear him, that means he'll be able to hear us."

He thought about that then cursed.

"All right." He tossed the covers back and got out of bed. "You get the aspirin and some bottled water and I'll check on my brother."

He walked to the master bedroom wearing only his T-shirt and underwear, but Avery took the time to step into her jeans. Her sexy, butt-hugging jeans.

If Seth hadn't interrupted them, they would have made love. And if they'd dated like two normal people instead of just falling into bed, he was sure they'd *be in love* right now. Because he was absolutely positive that was what was happening between them.

Even the fact that they'd found a house they both liked, albeit that it was Seth's, proved they were finding common ground. They were going to build a life together.

And he wasn't letting any of it to chance.

Avery drove the Porsche back to Seth's beach house and had to admit it was an amazing car. She put the top down and the air that spilled inside wreaked havoc with her hair, but she didn't care. For the first time since she got pregnant, she wasn't worried about Jake. Wasn't worried he'd find out about the baby and try to take it. Wasn't worried that he'd discover her dad's troubles. They were falling in love. For real.

Her life felt good. Wonderful.

She wasn't in the door of Seth's cozy bungalow two minutes before her phone rang.

Seeing it was Jake, she smiled as she answered, "Hey, you."

"How was the drive out?"

"Effortless. That car is fabulous. And now that I know I can handle it on the highway, I was thinking I should take a day and visit my parents."

Jake didn't say anything for a few seconds.

When he did speak, his voice had changed to cautiously optimistic. "If you're going to visit your parents, maybe it would be a good thing for me to go too."

Her heart caught. He wanted to meet her family and she wanted him to meet them. But she didn't want him to cut her visit short. She had things to do. She might be falling in love, but her life plan hadn't changed. She would be starting a law firm in Wilton. But she and Jake weren't at the place where they could talk about things like moving in together, let alone where they would live. And she couldn't take anything for granted. She had to go forward.

"Did you forget or not hear that I said I wanted to take a day? A *whole* day?"

"I can take a day."

She laughed. "Really?"

"Yes. You came to Paris with me to tell my mom about the pregnancy. I can take a day and introduce myself to your parents so they don't think the father of their grandchild is an unmitigated snob."

She winced. "I never told them you were a snob. I told them you were stuffy."

"So? I can be stuffy with them and meet or exceed their expectations."

She laughed again. "Stop. I just want you to be you."

His voice softened. "I can do that too."

He could. She knew that now. She also knew that he could surprise her and be funny, or kind, or understanding the way he was with Seth.

"We'll plan on tomorrow?"

"Sounds good."

She hesitated. It was on the tip of her tongue to ask him to stay at the beach house with her that night so they could get an early start, but she knew what would happen, and, honestly, there was a part of her that wasn't ready. She might have thrown caution to the wind at Seth's apartment, but now that things were really happening, her fears had reawakened.

He was still a rich guy, someone accustomed to getting everything he wanted. Her family had learned a huge lesson with Paul Barnes. Wealthy people didn't think the way average people did. They also used their power and influence to make sure they got what they wanted.

The overflowing emotions she had for Jake didn't mitigate or change the fact that they lived two different kinds of lives and wanted two different things out of life. They could laugh and play all they wanted. But at the end of the day, he was responsible not just for the family business but for his family.

And she wanted to change the world. Or at least her little corner of it. No matter how funny or friendly or downright happy they were, their lives would not easily mesh. One of them was going to have to make a huge compromise.

And she didn't think it could be her.

But maybe this trip would show them if it could be him?

"Okay, I'll see you tomorrow morning."

"You will."

"Bring doughnuts."

She disconnected the call to the sound of his laughter. But she also realized their trip to Wilton just might prove that he couldn't compromise any more than she could.

They were on the road the next morning by eight. He'd left his penthouse at four, with Gerry driving so he could work, and he arrived at the bungalow on time to eat two of the doughnuts he'd brought for breakfast. Then they headed for Pennsylvania.

Avery liked the Porsche so much that he kept the top down and they drove in the warm sunshine. She prompted him to take an exit a few miles past Allentown then directed him another couple of miles to the small town of Wilton. They glided along streets filled with quaint buildings and shops until they stopped at a ranch house.

After pulling up to the closed garage door, he turned to Avery. "That's not as far as I thought it would be."

She brightened. "I know!"

Thinking out loud, he added, "I bet it would be under an hour by helicopter."

An older woman raced from the front door before they could open their car doors. When Avery got out, she grabbed her and hugged her.

Jake exited the Porsche more slowly, examining the house and understanding why Avery loved Seth's bungalow so much, then looking at the short red-haired woman and taller bald man.

The man stepped forward, "I'm Dennis, Avery's dad. Everybody calls me Denny." He pointed to the woman who had her arm around Avery's waist. "That's Avery's mom, Andrea."

He said, "Hello," and shook both of their hands. As they walked into the small uncluttered home, he watched Denny in awe. This man had spent six years in prison for something he hadn't done, but you would never know it. In his jeans and sweatshirt, he was quiet and unassuming, but he had an easy laugh and a sparkle in his eye. He didn't appear bitter or angry. Just normal.

Avery's mom took her into the kitchen to get coffee and cake, but Jake could hear her grilling Avery about her pregnancy, whether she was taking care of herself. She seemed pleased to hear Avery had lost her job, then not so pleased to hear she was living in a beach house owned by Jake's brother.

"Why don't you come home?"

"My doctor's in the city," Avery casually replied. "Besides, I have a whole house to myself. I've got my Pennsylvania bar exam things scattered all over the dining room table. When I get hungry, I eat. When I get tired of studying, I go for a walk on the beach. Remember our beach trips, Mom?"

Andrea let out a long sigh. "Of course, I do."

"Seth's house is like one of the ones we used to rent. Except it has a big screen TV and a patio the size of Ohio."

Her mother laughed. "You always were one for exaggeration."

"And the beach is semiprivate so I'm not running into weirdos."

"That's always good."

Jake chuckled and Denny cleared his throat. "They could gab like that for hours."

Jake faced him. "Does Avery visit often?"

Denny shrugged. "In spurts. She loves it here in the summer, so when she doesn't have a lot of work to do, she's here on the weekends."

"It's not really a long drive."

"Depends on what you consider long."

"I've been traveling almost three hours to get to the beach house where Avery's living."

"You've been going there?"

"I don't exactly check up on her, but I do like to make sure she has everything she needs."

Denny laughed. "Good man."

The warmth of Denny's approval filled him. So, he pushed just a little bit more. "Have you and your wife ever been to the city?"

"Avery's dragged us there a time or two."

"You don't like it?"

He leaned close and whispered, "It's amazing. I love the restaurants. I could do without the shopping though."

Jake chuckled, fully understanding. "Have you ever been to a Knicks game?"

"Wanted to, but there never seems to be time."

"Maybe I could arrange for you to get tickets."

Denny seemed surprised. "That would be great."

"You tell me the next time you'll be in New York and I'll make sure there are tickets at the door for you."

Avery and her mom walked in. Avery held

a tray with four pieces of cake on it. Andrea held the tray with coffee and mugs.

"Hope you don't mind simple."

He glanced at her. "Simple?"

"Just plain plates for cake and mugs for coffee."

He laughed. "If the cake is good, I'd eat it with my fingers."

Andrea beamed.

The cake was delicious. So was lunch at the diner. As he expected, his choice of T-shirt and jeans got him through the town with minimal notice. Everyone noticed Avery, though. They stopped. Talked. Hugged her. And then shook his hand when she introduced him.

It was all easy and nice. There were a few residents who gave them sideways glances, but he suspected that had more to do with the fact that there were those in the town who didn't believe her dad was innocent.

But Avery didn't seem to care. She focused on the people she liked, the ones who liked her.

He glanced around as she chatted. This would make an exceptional place to bring a child for long visits, to give him or her the opportunity not merely to see, but also to experience the other side of life.

It wouldn't only be good for their child. It would be good for him too. He wanted to understand everything about Avery, and to enjoy a little peace and quiet himself a few times a year. Week-long visits to her parents would benefit all of them. And if there was an emergency in the city, a helicopter could get him there quickly.

Everything was working out perfectly.

It was time to call Pete Waters.

CHAPTER FOURTEEN

THEY RETURNED TO the beach house a little before dark. The Porsche roared onto the driveway in front of the two-car garage. Jake pressed the button that opened the doors and once the Porsche was parked, he closed them again.

She didn't think that strange until he followed her into the kitchen and tossed the keys onto the center island.

"Where's Gerry?"

"Probably at home with his family." He caught her gaze. "I thought I'd stay tonight."

The day before that suggestion would have made her think of all the things they still had to work out. But after the way he'd gotten along with her parents, made small talk with her friends and obviously liked her hometown, everything seemed right. She fit into his world. But more important, he fit into hers.

She walked over to him, slid her arms around his neck and kissed him. "I'll need a shower first."

He tightened his arms around her waist. "How about if we shower together?"

She laughed. "That sounds like a great idea."

He kissed her deeply, wonderfully, and she melted into him. The kiss went on and on, an expression of pure emotion. Then he picked her up and carried her to the bedroom.

An hour later, sated and happy, clean and dry, she snuggled close to Jake in the big king-size bed of the bungalow's master bedroom, unable to believe how lucky she was.

Pressed against his side, she felt him take a long breath.

She sat up. "Are you okay?"

"Yeah. Probably more okay than I've ever been in my life."

"But?"

"I'm wondering how much I missed."

"Missed?"

"With you—" He glanced at her. "With *us*, things just happen. Even the way we found each other on Valentine's Day. Most of what we've done hasn't been planned and it's been remarkable."

"This really is the first time something like this has happened to you?"

"When I was a kid, I was too afraid to just let things happen. I was also constantly trying to stay one step ahead of my dad. Then, when I went to work for him I had to watch him like a hawk."

"You had good reason."

"I totally changed the company's reputation."

She lay back down and nestled against him. "So now you can relax."

"Part of me is afraid I won't be a good father because I didn't have a good father."

"Are you kidding? I'm guessing you've been more of a dad to Seth than your father ever was."

He stayed quiet.

"Jake, a lot of it comes naturally. We're going to see our little boy or little girl and just melt like two sticks of butter."

He laughed. "You have the best ways of phrasing things."

She tapped his chest. "And you have a whole lot of love in that heart beating in there. All a child wants is to be loved."

"The way your parents loved you?" He took another breath. "I had a short chat with your dad. He had no complaints about you. Nothing he'd change."

She thought about that. Though she had no doubt Maureen loved her children, she loved them a little differently than the way Avery's parents loved her. Easily. Naturally. No strings attached. No work required.

"That's sort of the key to parenting. Just to love your child exactly as he is and guide him through the tough stuff."

"I really liked your parents."

"They liked you too."

"And your small town."

Her heart skipped a beat. She'd seen the way he'd looked around. But more than that, she'd seen how easily he'd gotten comfortable. He might not be ready to say the words, but he could live there. She could already picture it.

"It's a beautiful place. I can understand why you love it so much."

"It was a great place to grow up."

"I'll bet. That park was amazing."

Part of her wanted to say, *So that's why I think we should live there*. But it was still too soon. They'd dated three weeks in the winter but had only gotten to know each other in the past two weeks.

She couldn't ask him to move for her any more than he could ask her to move for him.

"I'm not sure if this is good timing or bad but I have another charity ball on Saturday." He shifted so he could see her face. "I want you to go with me."

"To announce to the world that this is your baby?"

"I think the world got that point when the

tabloid printed our picture, remember? It's why we had to race to France."

She smiled at the memories. "If I'm going, I'm wearing the same dress I wore to the ball in Paris."

He shrugged. "I don't care. You looked stunning in that dress."

"I did." She laughed. "I'm not vain. It's just not easy to find a dress that looks that good when you're six months pregnant."

"Getting close to seven," he agreed, his voice filled with something that sounded like awe.

She knew exactly what he felt. Her skin virtually sparkled from the light of happiness glowing inside her. It wasn't all from the baby. It was from him. He'd gone from being stuffy and bossy to easygoing and happy. And now he talked. Not only about little things. About everything.

Though she knew the pregnancy had begun his metamorphosis, she'd like to think she'd been the one to make him happy, that a little bit of compromise had taken them a long way. Sure, they needed more time to cement what they felt. And after that there were tons more compromises to make. But from the way he'd reacted to her parents and to Wilton, she knew everything would work out.

* * *

The ball on Saturday night at the Waldorf turned out to be nearly a carbon copy of the one in Paris. The attendees and the language they spoke might be different, but the protocol was the same. Maureen walked with Avery and Jake through the receiving line, proud to have her son beside her and eager to introduce Avery as the mother of her soon-to-be-born grandchild. Like Jake, she didn't seem to mind Avery wore the same gown.

Of course, that could be because—with the exception of Annalise and Julianna—the people who saw her wear it the first time were across an ocean.

Still, everything was perfect, wonderful.

They danced the entire first set of songs without even once returning to the table. They had just finished a dance and were laughing when the band announced their break. As they walked to their seats, Jake slid his arm around her waist and she leaned into him.

Annalise sighed. "You're such a lovely couple."

Maureen sniffed. "They are, but it looks like one half of that couple is getting tired."

She was, but she didn't want to leave. She couldn't believe how easily she'd gotten adjusted to his life, his mother, attending parties littered with the rich and famous. But it was more proof that with a little compromise they fit.

"Let's stay for another couple of dances."

"Okay by me."

They danced the night away, then went back to his penthouse and made love. Jake fell into a sound sleep almost immediately but it didn't bother her. When they were dating he had been the lightest sleeper on the planet. It was as if he had been so bogged down by worry that he never totally relaxed. Now he slept. Peacefully. Easily.

She wanted to take the credit for that too.

The baby moved and she waited for him to stop, but he didn't. Not only did he roll around as if doing somersaults, but he kept her wide awake. Not wanting to disturb Jake she eased out of bed.

Chilled, she shrugged into a huge robe she found in his dressing room and padded toward the kitchen. She poured herself a glass of milk and made a peanut-butter-and-jelly sandwich and headed to his office.

He'd used her computer on the flight to Paris so she decided it was okay to use his. Like his documents, her notes for the bar exam were available through off-site storage, and rather than waste this whole night, she would use it to study.

She slipped into the office where his laptop sat open on a polished oak desk. She knew he'd worked on it that afternoon but was surprised he hadn't turned it off. She hit the Enter key to wake it up, only to discover an email from Pete Waters was up on the screen. She raised her hand to minimize the email, but as she did, she saw her name.

Oh, now she really couldn't look at it.

If this was about their custody battle or even about the fact that they might not need one, she couldn't see this.

Except the words *pro bono* caught her eye.

This email was not about their custody battle.

But it was about her and...

The pro bono arm of Waters, Waters, and Montgomery?

She sat down, swallowing hard as she read the short email. A deal between Jake and Pete Waters. His family would sign a ten-year contract to retain Waters, Waters and Montgomery and the firm would agree to expand their pro bono arm any way *Avery* wanted.

So she would stay in New York City.

CHAPTER FIFTEEN

JAKE AWAKENED THE NEXT morning and rolled over to hug Avery, but she was gone. He got out of bed, slipped into the pajama bottoms he'd carelessly flung halfway across the room the night before and walked out to the kitchen.

She wasn't there.

"Avery?"

He strolled through the hall, into the empty living room and finally headed for the office. He found her sitting at the desk, but facing the view of the skyline outside the huge penthouse window.

"Why would you be making a deal for me to work with Waters, Waters and Montgomery?"

His heart sank. Not because he didn't want her to know, but because all of this was happening the wrong way. The most unromantic way. And he'd wanted his proposal to be something she remembered for the rest of her life.

He took a few steps into the room. "It was all part of a marriage proposal."

She swiveled the chair around, her expression horrified. "Getting me a job was part of your marriage proposal?"

He laughed. "No. Well, sort of. After I'd asked you to marry me—" He walked over to a bookcase, removed three fat volumes and revealed a wall safe. With a few twists of a dial, he had the door open. He took out the jeweler's box.

She bounced out of the chair. "Don't even ask!" Her eyes filled with tears that quickly spilled over. "I've spent the biggest part of my life preparing to take my place in the world, as an advocate for people who fall through the cracks."

"And you can do that at Waters, Waters and Montgomery." He stopped, his heart simultaneously crashing and filling with fear. "Sweetheart." He struggled to keep his voice from sounding desperate. He'd genuinely figured out the best compromise position, yet she didn't see it. "I have to stay in New York. You can be more flexible. This works for us."

"More flexible?" She should have looked small and helpless in his huge robe. Instead, she looked regal, strong. "I thought after our visit to Pennsylvania, you saw another compromise. One that actually required you to bend a little."

His face scrunched in confusion. "You thought I was considering moving to Pennsylvania?"

Her chin lifted. "It's not such a stretch. An hour helicopter ride to the city, remember? But really, that's not the issue." She reached across the desk, turned his laptop toward him. "This is a finalization memo. There had to have been discussions. Meetings. Other emails. Planning." She caught his gaze. "You did all this without ever once consulting me."

His heart did a silly thing, like a rumba that combined his fear that her anger was too great to pacify and a horrible, horrible feeling that he was like his dad, had done something his father would have done. Easily. Without thought that it was wrong. Because he didn't think it was wrong. He saw it as right. Just as his dad always did.

"I…" He swallowed.

Why hadn't he told her?

Because he wasn't accustomed to consulting anyone.

Why wasn't he accustomed to consulting anyone?

Because he was the boss.

Like his dad.

No! He'd fought that and won. This was just the overplanner in him coming out again.

"I know this is going to sound like an excuse but, honestly, I'm accustomed to doing things that I see need to be done. You've gotten me to stop planning, but I can't completely stop thinking ahead. I run a conglomerate. If I never planned, the companies would fall apart. Thinking ahead is what I do."

"Even if you're wrong?"

"This isn't wrong! You said yourself your original dream had been to get an education, find a high-powered job in New York and get an apartment in Paris. A second home."

She gaped at him. "That was the dream of a child. As I grew up, that dream changed into something more meaningful."

"And working for the pro bono arm of Waters, Waters and Montgomery, you'll have the more meaningful job. If you would take a few minutes and think it through, you would see this is right. This is the right answer."

"And if you would take a few minutes to think it through, you would see that if you think that's right, you don't know me at all. You don't know my heart. You don't know that I've worked all these years with a very specific goal in mind. To help my friends. My neighborhood. Not some equally worthy group of people that I don't know. But my friends." She walked up to him, caught his gaze. "Because I don't think you understand loyalty." Her eyes filled with tears again and she swallowed. "I don't think you understand friendship or community." She swallowed again. "Or love. All you see is what you want. What you need."

With that she brushed past him.

He let her go. He had to. What she said was the truth. He thought he loved her. But she was right. He couldn't love her if he didn't know her. If he'd truly known her, he would have realized a job in New York might appease her but it wouldn't satisfy her.

He was so casually selfish that he didn't even see it in himself anymore.

His heart cracked as pain pummeled him. He'd lost the best thing he'd ever had because he was selfish.

Avery didn't pack, only changed clothes. Wearing jeans and a T-shirt, she stormed out of Jake's penthouse and was on the street in what felt like seconds.

She was glad he hadn't followed her. Her heart absolutely ached with grief. And not even for herself. But for him.

She'd seen from the look on his face that even after their conversation about how to love their baby, everything she'd told him about loving her had surprised him. He'd been born confident, privileged, believing everything he said and did was right because he only ever came at problems with one need in mind. His. Or his family's. Most often his family's.

She stood on the sidewalk, seven months pregnant, broken, with a hundred dollars in her wallet, two credit cards and a three-hour cab ride to Seth's beach house, and then she'd have to get herself and her belongings to Wilton.

She took a long breath to steady herself and called her dad. "Any chance you feel like a drive to the city?" She could leave her clothes behind, but eventually she'd have to go back to the beach house for her books and laptop. Today, however, was not that day.

Her dad answered sleepily, as if she'd awakened him. "Where are you?"

She hailed a cab. "I'm on my way to Broadway. Remember the hotel you and Mom loved."

"Yes."

"That's where I'll be. In front of that hotel."

Her dad's voice dipped. "Are you okay?"

"I'm fine." She struggled with a sob that wanted to erupt and grief that cut the whole way to her soul, but she said, "Really. I'm just not staying at the beach house anymore."

A taxi finally stopped. She glanced back at

Jake's building, realizing she'd given him at least five minutes to put on pants and come after her. But he hadn't. He was up in his ivory tower. Warm. Safe. Coddled.

If she'd accepted the form of love he wanted to give her, she'd be compromising for the rest of her life.

Compromising everything she wanted.

Because the rich didn't compromise. They took what they wanted.

So why did her heart hurt? Why did her chest feel anchored down with grief?

She drew a shaky breath as she reached for the door. "Gotta go, Dad. See you in front of the hotel."

"It's gonna be a couple of hours."

"It's Sunday. Traffic will be light. But even if it isn't, I'm fine. I'll get breakfast. Watch tourists. I'll be okay."

She thought that until the taxi left her off and she began looking for somewhere to eat. Then her knees began to shake and her heart shattered into a million pieces.

She could call Jake a snob all she wanted. She could recognize that he liked things his own way, that he pushed and manipulated, but deep down she knew he was a prisoner of his life.

And maybe he was right. Maybe he really didn't have choices.

* * *

Jake spent Sunday sitting in the chair where he'd found Avery that morning, staring out the office window the way she had been. Sunlight sparkled off the windows of high-rises. The sky was so clear and blue, he could see for miles.

The sun set. The moon rose. At one point, he told himself to get up off the chair and take a shower, but he didn't listen. He just sat there.

Monday morning, he called Seth and told him he wouldn't be in to work that day. Then he hung up the phone so Seth couldn't ask why.

Tuesday, he actually showered but didn't dress beyond sweats and a T-shirt. What had happened with Avery, everything she'd said, became an endless loop in his brain, taunting him one minute, tormenting him the next.

Wednesday, he drove to the beach house but she wasn't there. Neither were her things. Seth phoned that afternoon to tell him that she'd returned the keys, and though Jake said, "Thanks for letting me know," a shockwave went through him.

What if she'd come to the office hoping to see him?

When his heart rate picked up and his hope restored at just the possibility, he ran his hand across his mouth.

Loving her wasn't helping him. It was ruining him. He hadn't been to work in days. He'd abandoned Seth in his time of grief. And God only knew what his mother was up to.

He called Gerry.

As Gerry drove him to the office, he called his mom. She chatted on about things that should change in the city, projects she wanted him to take on, and he saw his calendar fill up with meetings he'd need to hold. It rattled through him that his life always seemed to be dictated by somebody else. It rattled through him that all his free time was now gone. It rattled through him that he'd probably never find real love again.

But lots of people in life were given worse destinies. He would step into his.

When he arrived at work, his office quickly filled with assistants and vice presidents. He didn't blink. He handled everything.

The mess cleared around six, when everyone either had their question answered or had an appointment to see him the next day. A half hour later, Seth poked his head in the door.

"I see the thundering herd is gone."

He nodded, eager to talk to his brother and help him too. "Come in." He motioned for him to take a seat. "How are you feeling?"

Seth's eyes filled with sadness. "The shock wore off and the grief that followed was brutal."

"I can only imagine."

"How are *you* feeling?"

He shook his head as if he didn't understand the question. "I'm fine."

"Avery looks like hell."

His head snapped up. "Does she look sick?"

"More like worn and tired."

Hearing that, he pulled himself together again. "It's part of pregnancy. Her mother will make sure she gets sufficient rest."

"*You* should be making sure she gets sufficient rest. I saw you two that morning at my apartment."

"You were so hungover you were probably also seeing unicorns and rainbows."

"You couldn't hide the looks that passed between you or the way you just sort of meshed."

He laughed. "Seriously? Meshed? The woman wants to live in Pennsylvania."

"What's wrong with Pennsylvania?"

"I belong here."

"Who says?"

"My job for one. Plus, Mom." He thought of the eight million things she wanted him to accomplish in the firm's name, took a breath and sighed. "It doesn't matter anyway. Avery accused me of manipulating her, but the truth is she was manipulating me too. Not overtly."

It made him feel odd to say that. Avery hadn't said one word about their situation. Adding himself to her trip to Pennsylvania had been his idea. And when he even thought something negative about her his heart hurt. So he stopped himself.

"You're really upset because she thinks you're controlling."

He raised his gaze to look at Seth. "I am controlling. I see the way a thing should go and move heaven and earth to get it there."

"It's why the company is successful. You made us honest again."

"Apparently, I wasn't honest with Avery. I just went to Pete Waters and made a deal for her to head his pro bono department."

"Without asking her?"

"I wanted to surprise her." He shook his head and closed his eyes. "I liked surprising her. Surprises made her happy. I thought the job with Pete would make her happy."

"You are really new at this love stuff."

Offended, he stiffened. "I've had girlfriends."

"We've all had girlfriends, but we don't always fall in love." His head tilted as he studied his brother. "It really did surprise you, didn't it?"

"I thought it was perfect."

"Nothing is perfect."

"Right."

"I'm serious." Seth studied him for a few seconds. "You don't miss her?"

"I'm happier when I'm angry with her, when I'm not thinking about how much fun we had. But you just disabused me of my perfectly acceptable excuse of thinking she manipulated me. And now all I can remember are the good times. So, I miss her again." He squeezed his eyes shut and let the hurt roll through him.

Seth laughed. "Jake, go after her. Compromise. Figure this out."

Jake gaped at his younger brother. "Look who's giving me advice. You haven't had a steady girlfriend in four years."

"Because I made a mistake. I let the woman I wanted get away."

Jake's face scrunched in confusion. "There was someone you were serious about?"

"I didn't even know it until it was too late." He glanced up at Jake. "And even then I think I could have fixed it. But I did the same thing as Dad. I sucked it up, told myself I was a Mc-Callan and it was her loss."

"The way he used to when a negotiation went bad."

"Exactly. I did that and I lost. Don't lose. Go after her."

He shook his head. "I can't. She didn't accept my proposal. She wouldn't even let me propose. Part of me knows she's right and the other part realizes that if she didn't like the deal I made with Pete Waters, then maybe she doesn't know me well enough to love me."

Seth sat back. "You really think that?"

"I don't know what to think."

"What do you want?"

He wanted to feel forever what Avery made him feel. He wanted fun dinners, relaxed afternoons, hot sex that was still warm and intimate. He wouldn't tell even one of those to his brother.

"I don't know."

"Have you ever really thought about it? I mean, being brought up as the guy to replace Dad never gave you a chance to figure out who you wanted to be."

He'd never looked at it that way, but he supposed that was true.

Seth rose. "Do me a favor. Before you write off the woman Mom thinks is absolutely perfect for you and I thought was cute and funny enough to give you a real run for your money… think about it. If you didn't have the shackles of this job, what would you be doing right now?"

CHAPTER SIXTEEN

AVERY GOT UP every morning at six, cried, then took a shower. The first day after she'd left New York, she'd quickly realized living with her parents in a three-bedroom ranch with one bathroom wasn't an option.

The next day, she'd busied herself with finding an apartment or rental house she could move into immediately and found a vacated Cape Cod that was for sale. It made her think of Maureen and she cried when she signed the purchase agreement, but she told the listing agent it was pregnancy hormones then spent an hour listening to Alice Johnson's pregnancy stories.

Because that's what life was about in a small town. And being a part of her community again would probably save her. She went to the post office, the diner and shopped at the grocery store for her mom, listening to stories, talking about the law firm she intended to start.

Though not many people needed a criminal lawyer, everybody had a tale about an estate settlement gone wrong, sexual harassment, a lease, a brother-in-law who'd borrowed money and hadn't paid it back...and suddenly she felt like Judge Judy.

She walked to the ranch house and told her parents she'd paid cash for the Cape Cod and would be moving in within a week. Though they were concerned about her living out the last months of her pregnancy alone, at the end of the week, once the deed had been recorded and her check had cleared, they helped her cart her boxes over.

Maureen called. Pretending to be chipper, Avery was glad to have the Cape Cod to talk about because it prevented awkward silences. She even gave her the address so she could send housewarming flowers.

Two days later, sitting on the floor of the empty living room—the purchaser of her condo now owned her living room furniture, dining room table and bedroom set—she looked around at the rest of her life.

Eventually, she would paint the dark wood-work white, install hardwood floors bleached and stained a pale gray and furnish the room with a white burlap sofa and chair with a bright print area rug and flowers on the mantel of the stone fireplace.

She'd remodel the kitchen and knock out a wall, so she could see her daughter or son playing in front of the fireplace on cold winter nights as she made soup.

The picture that formed brought tears to her eyes again. Jake should be in that picture too. Leaning over his laptop at the kitchen table, while he talked on the phone.

When the soup was ready, he'd say, "Sorry, gotta go. Dinner's on the table." Then he'd eat a real meal with her and their child. They'd do homework together, get the kid's bath together and read stories as a family. Because that's what he needed. A slice of real life. The chance to be himself.

But he'd never get it because controlling things until they were perfect, flawless, no chance of spilled milk or actual human contact had been ingrained in him.

She got up from the floor, stretched and let the baby move around, repositioning itself to be comfortable.

When the old-fashioned doorbell sent a loud buzz through the house, she winced, realizing that was another thing she'd have to change. And the sooner the better.

She wobbled to the door. A dark wood frame

housed beveled glass that had been pieced together like art. Two long rectangular pieces
stood like sentries on the right and left side,
while smaller pieces mixed and mingled to
make something that looked like a crystal
sunrise.

She was definitely keeping that.

She opened the door without thinking and
when she saw Jake standing on her wide front
porch with huge white columns, her mind went
blank.

"Hey."

He wore a black leather jacket over a T-shirt
and jeans and with a few days' growth of beard
he looked disreputable and sexy. Just normal
enough to be a good dad and just sexy enough
to be...*hers*.

Her hormones kicked in and she almost
started to cry, but she caught herself. This guy
was smart and savvy. And he was her child's
father. They'd never gotten around to discuss-
ing custody or visitation.

He could be here to determine just how
strong she was.

He could be here to negotiate.

He could be here to bully her...

Or manipulate her.

This wasn't the time for tears, or thinking
how plain old sexy he looked. This was the

moment she either protected her child from overexposure to everything money could buy, or started a never-ending battle with one of the most powerful families in the United States.

Just when she was ready for the worst, he pulled a bouquet of flowers from behind his back and handed them to her.

Her heart skipped a beat. Her thoughts scattered.

"These are from Mom. She said to tell you the vase is coming. It's Tiffany something or another. She ordered it hoping it would come to your house before the flowers died."

Her heart plummeted so fast, she wondered if she had any pulse at all. Of all the stupid things to do, jumping to the conclusion that he'd bought her flowers because he loved her, maybe wanted to compromise, was the stupidest, stupidest thing she had ever done.

She took the flowers. "Thank your mother for me." Then she shook her head. "No. Don't. I know my new protocol is to send an appropriate thank-you note."

She made a move to close the door, but he put his foot in it before she could.

She glanced up sharply. That was so not a Jake McCallan thing to do.

"In retrospect, giving you flowers from my mother was pretty dumb. I came here to apologize and ended up looking like a delivery guy."

The way he said that, as if making a mental note never to do it again, almost had her laughing. But she refused to let his charm get to her. Too much was at stake.

"If you want to talk about custody or visitation, save it for a hearing or a meeting with our lawyers. Tell Pete I hired Andi Petrunak as my legal counsel. Too much has passed between us for us to try to negotiate on our own."

He put his foot a little farther in the door. "That's actually why I'm here."

"I thought it was to apologize."

"It was. Then after the apology I was going to tell you that I love you."

Her heart flattened then swelled. "You've never said that before."

"And I'm not sure why. I've loved you since Paris. Knew it in my heart, just wanted to get all our ducks in a row before I said it."

"There's your problem," she said, her voice breaking with raw emotion. She loved this man in a way that encompassed so many things that she couldn't even name them. And he had to have every i dotted and t crossed before he could even hold a decent conversation. "You think too much. You want everything perfect—"

He reached in the door, caught her by the waist and hauled her to him, kissing her fiercely. She wrapped her arms around his neck and let him take her where he would. Not only did she like this side of him, but he needed to be able to live this side of himself freely.

He finally released her. "How's that for not thinking."

"You're getting the hang of it."

She said it so casually that he laughed. "I will figure all this out, you know."

"Don't!" she said, dragging him off her porch and into the small foyer then the empty sitting room. "Don't always do what you think you have to do. Do what you want to do."

"I can't spend my life not planning. It's not how I'm wired. But I did realize that I can't always plan alone."

"I'm listening."

"I knew what you wanted, but I thought that was what you wanted before we started... I think that's how I justified making big sweeping arrangements."

"You never thought to ask?"

He shook his head. "I wanted to surprise you. You like surprises. I didn't think it through." He winced. "I'm embarrassed to have to admit that."

"You should be."

"Hey, the whole love thing is new to me. Sharing my life is almost scary…except I love you. And when I'm not with you I'm empty."

Tears filled her eyes. He'd been so honest, so courageous, she had to be too. "I was lost without you too."

"So, what do we do?"

She smiled. He hadn't come up with a plan. Hadn't suggested what he wanted first. "You asked."

"I'm learning."

He really was. And her heart almost couldn't take it. "I think we need to be together."

"I do too." He looked around as she took the flowers to the kitchen table. "So, this is where we're going to live?"

Her breath caught and she whipped around to face him. "You're going to live here with me?"

He met her gaze. "I want to be with you. I also want you to be happy. And I think raising a child here would be fun."

"Yes. That's exactly how I see it."

"Except the house is small. It'll be good for a year or two, but if I'm working from home, I'll need a decent-sized office."

She pressed her hand to her chest. "You're working from home?"

"With new technologies, I've found a lot of things can be handled from home. I also trust my employees. I can also fly to New York a few times a week. But when I'm home, I'll need space."

"You can have space."

"We'll sit down with an architect as soon as the baby is born." He slid out of his jacket and hung it on the newel post. "But first we need dinner. Is there takeout in this town?"

Her heart skipped a beat. "Of course, there's takeout in this town."

"A bed upstairs?"

She winced. "Mattress."

He laughed. "This should be interesting."

She walked over, wrapped her arms around his neck. "That's the point. We are absolutely not going to have a dull life."

He smiled. "No. We're not."

Then he kissed her again, and he knew with absolute certainty that this was what he'd been searching for his entire life. Not surety. Not perfection. But something warm and sweet, hot and sexy, smart and strong, naughty and nice.

Avery.

EPILOGUE

Jake leaned against the window seat in Avery's hospital room, watching his mother cuddle his daughter, her first grandchild. Abigail Maureen McCallan. Apparently, all the women in Avery's mother's family had names that started with *A*, so that took care of naming her after someone in the Novak family. And his mother unashamedly said if she got to pick the middle name she wanted it to be Maureen.

They hadn't waited for the baby's birth to hire an architect and plans for their bigger house were nearly complete. Avery was just about ready to take the Pennsylvania bar exam. And no one seemed to care he wasn't in the office three days a week.

Nestling the baby against her breast, his mom said, "You know, Avery and I saw the cutest wedding dress in Paris." She smiled. "She even tried it on."

"You did?"

"Your mother tricked me into thinking it was an ordinary ball gown. As soon as I put it on, I knew it wasn't." She sighed wistfully. "But it certainly was gorgeous."

Maureen nodded. "Yes, it was." She handed Abigail to Avery's mother. "As soon as Avery can travel, we'll go to Paris together and you can take a look."

Andrea's face fell. "I can't go to Paris."

Maureen batted a hand. "It's not a big deal. We have a plane. And I have a sweet deal with a hotel there. I can get a suite for the three of us for next to nothing."

Andrea brightened.

Jake stifled a gasp. She didn't have a sweet deal. She paid top dollar and was proud of it. But Andrea didn't have to know that.

Sabrina and Seth entered. Sabrina walked directly to Avery and hugged her. Seth carried a huge teddy bear.

Avery laughed. "I don't think the nursery is big enough for that."

Jake shook his head. "I don't think our current house is big enough for that."

Seth slapped him on the back. "Luckily, you're building a new one." He paused. "There is going to be a room for me, right?"

"Two spare bedrooms and a mother-in-law suite," Avery said.

"But don't get too comfortable in the spare bedrooms," Jake put in. "We want to fill them with kids."

"We're thinking of building a bed-and-breakfast in town."

"I'm going to run it," Denny said, pushing away from the wall. "Andrea's going to bake goodies for guests."

Sabrina smiled. "That sounds like a great idea. That way we can visit and not feel like we're intruding." She paused, then gave Jake a narrow-eyed look. "You did that on purpose, didn't you?"

Jake pointed at his temple. "Always thinking."

Andrea shifted to hand the baby to Seth. "Here. Hold her."

He jumped back. "Oh, no. I've never held one of those in my life and don't plan on starting now. I'll hold her when she's two. Or three. Or maybe I'll just introduce myself when she's seven and can play catch."

Avery and her mother laughed. But Maureen frowned and faced Andrea. "See why I despaired of being a grandmother?"

"At least you had a shot. I had a daughter who wanted to save the world and a son who ran into burning buildings."

"Hey, I gave you a grandchild," Avery said

with a laugh, but Jake could see her energy was waning.

He rose from the window seat. "I think it might be time for us to let Avery get some rest."

Seth said, "Aw. I just got here."

But Andrea and Maureen were already herding people toward the door.

He'd never seen his mother like this, not just happy but involved.

When everyone was out of the room, he sat on the seat next to the bed and took Avery's hand. "You okay?"

"I'm fine." She winced. "I don't think the drugs have worn off yet."

"Which might explain why you're tired."

"That and ten hours of labor."

He laughed. "That too."

"Little tip. Never tell a woman in labor that you understand her pain." She cut him a look. "You don't."

"Point taken."

"So, you're happy with a girl?"

He laughed. "I'm going to be the most possessive, protective father ever. I've already got plans for upping the security system on the new house."

"Sounds good." She yawned. "Next time, I'm going into labor in the morning instead of eleven o'clock at night."

"Just go to sleep."

The words were barely out of his mouth before her eyes closed. Within seconds, she was out.

He took a breath, rose from the chair beside the bed and walked over to the bassinette.

His little girl was tiny. Only two ounces over five pounds. She had the McCallan trademark black hair and blue eyes but green-eyed Andrea had reminded them that all babies had blue eyes and when she was about a year old they'd know the real color.

He reached down and tucked the mitten over her hand more securely. Any fear he might have had had disappeared. Not because he had planned or prepared for this—but because he was ready for the adventure.

In fact, with Avery, he was looking forward to it.

* * * * *

*Look out for the next romance story in the
Manhattan Babies trilogy*

Coming soon!

*And if you enjoyed this story,
check out these other great reads
from Susan Meier*

The Spanish Millionaire's Runaway Bride
The Boss's Fake Fiancée
A Mistletoe Kiss with the Boss
Wedded for His Royal Duty

All available now!

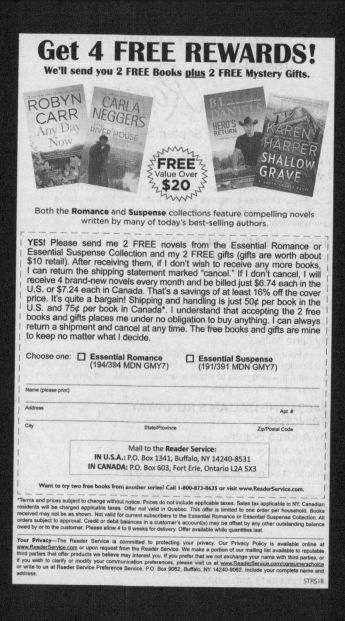